Jinxed!

Jinxed!

Adapted by Robin Wasserman

Based on "The Partner" and "The Rep"
Teleplays by Laura McCreary and Chris Nee
Based on *Unfabulous* created by Sue Rose

SCHOLASTIC INC.

New York   Toronto   London   Auckland   Sydney
Mexico City   New Delhi   Hong Kong   Buenos Aires

ISBN 0-439-83158-X

12 11 10 9 8 7 6 5 4 3 2 1   6 7 8 9 10/0
Printed in the U.S.A.
First printing, February 2006

Jinxed!

I don't like science class. And you know what? It doesn't like me. It never has — and this year has been worse than ever:

When our science teacher, Ms. Gonzales-Menendez-Mendoza, handed back our latest set of pop quizzes, we could tell from the look on her face that the results weren't going to be pretty. As I waited to get my quiz back, I kind of hoped that she had lost it. I didn't really want to see the grade — it was just too depressing.

"The results of your last quizzes were less than stunning," Ms. Gonzales-Menendez-Mendoza said drily as she passed back the last of them. That's her way. She starts off slow and kind of quiet, and then inevitably . . . "Or as my father, *Doctor Gonzales-Menendez,* would say —"

BAM!

She slapped her hands down on someone's desk and started shouting at us in rapid-fire Spanish: "You pathetic group of brainless fools! You wouldn't know science if it bit you!" (We got the translation later on. The kid who sits next to me speaks fluent Spanish.)

See what I mean? It's a slow burn. She starts off calm, but by the time she's done with us, it's like someone lit her hair on fire. She set her mouth in a firm, angry line and paced through the classroom, slamming the quizzes down on people's desks. I got a special glare as she passed mine back — it didn't seem like a very good sign.

She pounded the quiz down on my desk with a thud and strode quickly away to deliver her next piece of bad news. I slunk down in my seat and slowly lifted the top right corner of the page, peeking underneath it. I was afraid to look.

And with good reason: I got a D. This was *not* good.

"Fortunately, you'll all have a chance to bring up your grades by participating in the science fair!" Ms. Gonzales-Menendez-Mendoza told us, a note of encouragement suddenly present in her voice.

But I wasn't encouraged. I was more deflated than ever. *Science fair.* Why do they try and make it sound so pleasant? I mean, calling it a "fair" just makes you think of a fabulous carnival with rides, games, and lots of cotton candy. You picture everyone riding carousels and winning pie-eating contests. But what do you get instead? A crowded room full of lame posters and stinky, leaky beakers — and if you're me, Addie Singer, a surefire chance to make a fool of yourself in front of a bunch of judges and all of Rocky Road Middle School!

If you ask me, they should call it "science misery" instead.

"As usual, the winning project will represent Rocky Road at regionals," Ms. Gonzales-Menendez-Mendoza reminded us, as if I could have forgotten this nightmare from when we went through it last year, "where my father, Dr. Gonzales-Menendez, is a judge. Try not to embarrass me, people."

Please. I'm way too busy trying not to embarrass myself. No matter how hard I try, or who I have as a partner, the science fair is *always* a disaster.

Exhibit A: two years ago, when my partner and I decided to build a model volcano. No big deal, right? Standard science fair project, guaranteed to be a winner. Too bad *I'm* guaranteed to be a loser. We built our model, brought it to the fair, and when the time came, I slipped on my goggles and pushed the switch.

Nothing happened.

I pushed the switch again.

Still nothing.

So I bent over and looked inside the volcano to figure out what was going on . . . and *that's* when it exploded, splattering my face and clothes with gooey red "lava." Well, it was actually molasses plus red food coloring. And guess what. Turns out that kind of stain never washes out.

We didn't win.

Exhibit B: The year after that, I tried to take it easy. My partner and I did a project about growing plants. Nothing can backfire there, right? No disasters waiting to happen, no explosions or anything — I mean, all we had to do was take care of a potted geranium. We did a great job, and our flower was doing so well . . . until we brought it to the fair. As the judges lined up in front of our booth, my partner set out the flower, and I switched on the heat lamp — and our geranium blew up. No, literally, it just burst into smoke. Scientifically impossible? Trust me, nothing's impossible when you're me. I'm jinxed.

Anyway, after last year, I had made a promise to myself: *No more science fair.* So I timidly raised my hand and waited for Ms. Gonzales-Menendez-Mendoza to call on me. She did, but only after she'd come over to my desk. I looked up at her, towering over me, and tried not to be too intimidated by her glare.

"Um. What would happen . . ." I began hesitantly. "What would happen if, like, someone skipped the science fair?"

Ms. Gonzales-Menendez-Mendoza narrowed her eyes. "Well, this someone would receive a zero that would be averaged into the rest of their grade. So, conceivably, if *someone* were doing well enough, they could take the hit." I started to smile — so it wasn't all bad news. Maybe there was a loophole.

"In your case, however . . ." She paused and tapped the D at the top of my quiz.

"But you don't understand," I protested. "I just . . . can't do science fairs. It's like I'm jinxed or something."

Ms. Gonzales-Menendez-Mendoza shook her head in bemusement and walked away. You could already tell she didn't believe me. No adult ever does. They think I'm just not trying hard enough or something. They don't get that these are powerful forces totally beyond my control.

"As a student of science," Ms. Gonzales-Menendez-Mendoza chided me, "I can assure you, there's no such thing as a jinx. You'll be fine. You just need to find a partner who can help you out."

A good partner, that's all I needed. Just one little problem — as soon as she said that, everyone in the classroom scooted their desks away from me and looked off in the opposite direction. And can I really blame them? Who would want to work with someone who was fated for disaster? For utter science fair catastrophe?

Who would want to work with someone who was jinxed?

As soon as I got out of class, I realized that I shouldn't have worried about finding a science fair partner. In my moment of panic, I'd totally forgotten that my two best friends in the whole world, Geena Fabiano and Zach Carter-Schwartz, were both in my class. Surely one of them would be willing to help me out . . . right?

"So, Geena," I began hopefully as we walked down the hall toward our lockers. "About science fair —"

"Sorry, Addie." She winced, and I could tell she'd been waiting in fear for me to bring it up. "I'm going to be partners with Julian from the art lab. I've decided that it doesn't matter what your project is — as long as your display is eye-catching enough, you'll pass." So Geena was out — no biggie. After all, that's why I have *two* best friends. You never know when you're going to need a spare!

"Zach?" I turned to him, my eyes filled with hope.

"I'd help you out, Addie, but you know . . ." Zach shrugged helplessly. "Randy Klein and I are airtight. You can't split up the dream team."

"Speaking of the dream team," Geena said, nodding toward the other side of the hallway where Patti Perez and Jake Behari were walking side by side, holding hands. Patti Perez was the most popular girl in school and leader of a clique of other popular girls. Jake Behari was . . . well, just the coolest guy I'd ever met in my life. So I guess it shouldn't have surprised me that they were partnered up. But it didn't make me feel any better.

"We could study the effects of moisture on various breeds of grass," I could hear Jake suggesting. "What do you think?"

"Yeah, sure." Patti shrugged and examined her manicure. "Whatever."

"Unless you had a better idea," he added.

"Yeah, sure, whatever."

Zach and Geena both spun their heads to look at me, waiting for some kind of reaction from me. I mean, of course I didn't like seeing Jake and Patti, but I had bigger things to worry about at the moment. So I just shrugged and pretended I didn't care. Hey, it was almost true.

"Over it," I told them.

Geena nodded firmly. "Good."

"Look, Addie," Zach said, his mind still on the science fair, "maybe you can find a new kid who doesn't know about your . . . track record."

"You mean the jinx," Geena put in helpfully. Thanks, Geena.

"I'm not jinxed," I protested in indignation. "I'm just . . . scientifically impaired. Besides, I have a plan." And it was true, I'd just come up with one. "Duane Ogilvy. He's a genius, right?"

"If you discount his social skills, fashion sense, and bizarre penchant for corn dogs, then sure, I guess," Geena agreed.

"I figure if I get him to be my partner, maybe I won't totally screw up this year." As I heard the words coming out of my mouth, I decided that this might be the best idea I'd had in a long time. Duane Ogilvy was weird, but he was also brilliant — so who better to help me pass?

"Zach, what are you and Randy doing?" Geena asked, now that my problem was — sort of — solved.

Zach shrugged. "All depends on what the St. Agnes girls are doing." I should probably mention that

Zach gets really . . . *intense* when it comes to the science fair. He and Randy Klein have been working together for years. Each year, they come really close to winning the whole thing — and each year, a team from St. Agnes beats them out for the top prize. I think Zach's almost as sick of losing as I am of being jinxed.

"You know why those St. Agnes girls win every year?" Geena asked.

"Because they cheat?" Zach suggested. You could tell he was only half joking.

"Because the matching uniforms present a visual united front to the judges," Geena explained. Of course, this fit in perfectly with her theory that the presentation was more important than the content. Geena wants to be a fashion designer — and actually she's already pretty good at making her own clothes. So you can see why she might want to believe that what you wear can affect what happens to you. Zach and I weren't so sure. "Gives the impression that they have excellent teamwork skills."

"This year, Randy Klein and I are totally gonna beat St. Agnes at regionals," Zach swore.

"Matching plaid outfits?" Geena asked. She was probably hoping she'd get to design them.

Zach shook his head grimly.

"Spy tactics."

"There he is," I said eagerly, marking my prey. Geena, Zach, and I were hanging out in *Juice!*, our favorite café, and I'd just spotted the guy I had been looking for all day long.

"Who?" Zach asked, spinning around in his seat. "Randy?"

"Duane," I corrected him. I stood up, and hoped that I looked like the kind of person you'd want to do a science fair project with. "I'm gonna go talk to him."

Duane was sitting across the café, whispering something to Mary Ferry. They made the perfect couple — they were both saddled with oversize eyeglasses, and their various quirks perfectly complemented one another. Mary was into the school paper; Duane was into insects, computers, and *Star Wars*.

"Addie, wait," Geena cautioned me, grabbing my wrist and pulling me back down. "You can't just go talk to him. You need to formulate your pitch. Figure out the pros and cons. Pro —" She stopped and thought for a moment. "You're cute. Con: You're jinxed."

Good point. So I sat there and tried to think — what else did I have going for me?

Just then, Zach's cell phone rang, totally interrupting my concentration.

"Randy!" Zach cried — he'd been looking for his partner-to-be all day. "What's up?"

"Had a mishap at St. Agnes," Randy moaned. "Fell out a window." I guess the "spy tactics" to find out what the St. Agnes girls were doing for the science fair had already begun. We could all hear Randy's tinny voice coming out of the phone — but even if we hadn't heard it, we could have guessed what he was going to say. Randy's kind of klutzy. I mean, I know I fall down a lot, but Randy's falls usually land him in the hospital, bundled up in a few layers of plaster. It's incredible — last year he broke a fifty-year-old record for most days of school missed by a single student!

"Wow, that's terrible," Zach said brusquely. It didn't sound like he was that interested in hearing the details of Randy's latest crash. "What projects are they doing?"

"Ambulance . . . on . . . the way," Randy groaned.

"Randy?!" But the line was dead.

"What'd he say?" I asked, pretending I didn't already know.

Zach sagged in his seat. "He says I'm gonna need a new science fair partner."

I beamed — this was like the best timing ever.

11

Well, you know, not that poor Randy Klein fell out another window. But if he was going to fall out a window, this was definitely the best time for him to do it. We found out later that luckily he'd landed on some bushes, but Randy was definitely out of the science fair.

"Zach, that's perfect!" I gushed. "You and I can —"

But Zach had disappeared from the table. Like lightning he'd bolted over to Duane Ogilvy's table as soon as he snapped the cell phone shut.

"So, since I'm the best and you're the second best, I'm thinking partners," he said, shooting Duane an oily grin. "Whaddaya say?"

Whaddaya say? How about what *I* say? And I say — traitor! Not only was Zach refusing to partner with me, but he was stealing *my* plan, and my potentially perfect partner! Unbelievable.

Duane, who doesn't have people like Zach begging him for help every day, was clearly enjoying the moment. He sipped his smoothie and furrowed his brow, as if he were really thinking hard about the possibility.

"Have you tried these new papaya smoothies?" he finally asked. "They're seasonal. Sip?" He held the glass out to Zach, who knocked it away in frustration.

"No, man! Will you be my partner or not?"

I held my breath, waiting for Duane to give Zach an answer. If he said yes, then my science fair future was totally sunk.

"Easy, tiger," Duane said. "Look, truth is, Mary and I have agreed to take our compatibility to a new level as science fair partners."

Uh-oh. Of course, I couldn't help but smile a little at the horrified look on Zach's face. But still, it looked like Duane wouldn't be partners with either of us. Which meant that I was still partnerless. And still jinxed.

"Come on," Zach whined. He never knows when to give up. "Duane, I'm sure Mary's a good —"

"Great," Duane corrected him.

"Right. Great friend, but this is *science fair*," Zach reminded him. "It's all about the win."

"Zach, I want to share this experience with some- one I think is great," Duane explained, gazing into Mary's eyes. "You should do the same." He turned away from Zach and took another sip from his smoothie.

Zach trudged back to our table and sat down, as if nothing had happened. He didn't even look ashamed of himself.

"Traitor," I spit out, giving him the stink eye. "Backstabber. Duane stealer."

Zach was completely unfazed. "Addie, I can't talk about this right now. I have to find a science fair partner."

"But — I —" I waved my hands in front of his face. Was I invisible or something? Did he not see that there was a perfectly good potential partner sitting right in front of him? And didn't I get some bonus points for being his best friend? "Hello!"

But Zach just gave me a friendly wave back — and then he took off. In search of a "better" partner, I guess. Did I mention he's a traitor?

I sighed, and Geena patted me on the shoulder sympathetically.

"I think he meant a partner who can actually win."

At least I've got one friend who's — wait a second, *"a partner who can actually win"*?

"Hey!" I protested.

But Geena just gave me a weak smile, and I could tell she agreed with Zach. And I guess, deep down, I wondered if she was right. After all, why should Zach want to work with me, if it meant he'd be destined to lose.

I pushed my drink across the table — I didn't want it anymore. It's hard to enjoy a cool, sweet Orange-tastic smoothie when you're thinking of yourself as a big fat loser.

14

The next night was my mom's birthday. And, as usual, I wrote her a song to commemorate the occasion.

She can stand on her head, she can cook for ten!
If she hadn't been born, there'd be no me or Ben!
She's Mom. She's Mom.
She's the bomb. Yeah   she's Mom.

Mom, Dad, and my brother, Ben, all clapped for me, and my mom tipped her party hat in my direction.

"Happy birthday, Mom," I told her, putting away my guitar.

"I can't believe you wrote me a song!" she gushed. It was sweet of her, but since I've written a song for her last five birthdays, it didn't seem like she could be that surprised. But every year, she pretends to be just as shocked and impressed — I guess that's what makes her such a great mom.

"Here," Ben said, handing her a card. "Happy birthday."

"Ben!" Mom exclaimed, opening the card. This time she really was surprised, and no wonder — Ben had never gotten her a card before. Or, at least, not since he was six years old.

"Eh, no big," he said, stepping out of the room to get phase two of Mom's present. "It's just a gift certificate to *Juice!*. All the employees get 'em at the end of the month."

Ben came back into the kitchen, holding a cake that was overflowing with candles.

"But I made you a cake," he said. There was a pause. "Actually, I bought it."

"And you even put the exact number of candles on it," Mom said, shrinking away from the heat. "How . . . thoughtful."

She took a deep, deep breath and then blew out as hard as she could — and even with a whole box of candles stuck into the cake, she managed to blow out all the flames.

"Did you make a wish?" I asked.

"I have a lovely family, good health, a beautiful

home," Mom said, with a blissed-out grin. "What could I possibly need?"

That's when Dad pulled a wrapped box out from under the table. "I can think of something," he said mischievously.

Mom bit her lip, but she took the present and began to unwrap it. Ben and I exchanged a nervous glance. Here's the thing: Dad is great at just about everything . . . except for giving gifts to Mom.

There was the giant porcelain turtle.

The red feather-trimmed sweater. Or was it a skirt? Or was it a nightgown? We could never figure it out   there were too many feathers.

And who could ever forget the year Dad gave her the combination lamp and teapot? ("So you can see what you're pouring," he'd said, "even in the dark.") None of us knew what he was thinking that time. Of course, none of us ever do.

I'm pretty sure Mom would prefer that Dad never buy her another present again. But of course, she's way too nice to say so. And so every year, she puts on her brightest smile and pretends to love whatever it is he bought.

"Oh, honey, you didn't have to," she said as she was opening the box, her fake smile already firmly plastered to her face. She's gotten pretty good at it after all these years.

"No, no," Dad protested. "I know I maybe haven't picked the best gifts in the past, but this year, I did my research. Prepare to be thrilled."

Mom looked surprised, and even slightly hopeful — she was willing to take Dad at his word. After all, he was so enthusiastic, so sure of himself, and just because every other year he'd given her an atrocious present didn't mean that this year . . .

"Oh." Mom's face fell a bit as she pulled the heavy, bulky object out of the box. "A kissing-fish cookie jar," she observed. Her voice was flat, but I could tell she was trying to look and sound grateful. It would just take a minute.

"And there's a surprise inside, once you get through all the cookies!" Dad told her, so eager that he was practically bouncing up and down.

"Ha! Good one, Dad!" Ben said. He was laughing so hard he could barely get the words out. "Where's her real gift?"

"Ben. This *is* her real gift," Dad said, puzzled.

Mom shot Ben a warning look, then gazed up at Dad, composing her face to appear totally sincere and thankful.

"It's perfect," she lied — but for all the best reasons. "I love it."

"I know you do," Dad said smugly. "I saw that you'd been watching this cookie jar on the auction site, so I swooped in and bought it."

I almost gasped aloud. I'd been in the kitchen the day when Mom first discovered the kissing-fish cookie jar online. She couldn't stop laughing at it. And when she finally did stop laughing, she immediately called all her friends.

"Marcy, I'm sending you the link now," she'd giggled to our next-door neighbor. "Two people have actually bid on this thing. This is worse than that goose-for-all-seasons lawn ornament!"

I guess it's not very nice to make fun of other people's taste — but in this case, the punishment was definitely way more heinous than the crime!

Mom smiled weakly, and I could tell that she, too, was remembering that day in the kitchen. "How ... industrious of you," she told him, and gave him a big, warm hug.

Now *that's* true love.

In science class the next day, everyone was hard at work on their science fair projects. At one end of the room, Geena and Julian were huddled over their lab table, poring over a series of sketches.

"So we should talk lettering first," Geena suggested, holding up the piece of Julian's artwork she liked the best. "Something that really pops. I say either furry or metallic." Julian nodded, and Geena looked over her shoulder, shooting the competition a smug smile. She was already congratulating herself for choosing such a talented partner — as far as she was concerned, first prize was guaranteed. Even if they hadn't actually picked a project yet.

Julian pulled out his laptop, which was encased in a homemade cover of striped zebra fur.

"I like, I like," Geena said, petting the cover as if it were her new pet.

"Mmm," Julian mumbled. He didn't talk much. But that was okay. He was an artistic genius, after all. As Geena had explained to us the day before, she didn't need him to talk. She just needed him to produce.

On the other side of the room, Jake Behari was pouring drops of water onto a bunch of different chunks of sod.

"I'll take it home tonight, and you can take it home tomorrow," Jake murmured as he bent close to the measuring cup to make sure he was pouring out the right amounts.

Patti, intent on filing her nails, wore the same bored expression she's had since the third grade.

"No can do," she told him, not bothering to look up from her on-the-go manicure. "The gardener only comes Tuesdays and Fridays."

Jake didn't say anything out loud — but he didn't have to. His look was clear enough: *You've got to be kidding me.*

Patti finally looked up from her nails and smiled at Jake, shaking her head in mild exasperation. All of Patti's emotions are mild — she claims that wild facial expressions cause premature wrinkles.

"I know," she said as she heaved a sigh. "I wanted him three days a week, too. But my mom said it would be wasteful."

Since I was walking by on my way to Zach's table, I heard it all — but I stifled my laughter. It wouldn't be polite, not when Jake Behari was slumped back in his chair looking like he was up to his waist in quicksand and sinking fast. Not that he didn't deserve it, just a little — I mean, who would ever think Patti would make a good science fair partner? Sure, she was the most snobby girl in school — I figured that being snobby was a full-time job. It didn't leave much room for anything else, like homework, or speaking to her "inferiors" . . . or science fair.

I just shrugged my shoulders and kept going. I had problems of my own. At the top of the list: I still didn't have a partner! Zach was sitting alone, scouring a bunch of science magazines. As far as I could tell, he was still partnerless, too. And I was determined to make him see that we could be the perfect solution to each other's problems.

"Every project has been done," he moaned as I sat down. He barely seemed to notice I was there, and I wondered if, before I arrived, he'd been complaining to thin air. "There are no original ideas left in the world."

"Well, what if we —"

"Addie, there is no *we*," he reminded me sourly.

"Zach, come on. Your science fair skills will balance out my . . . streak of bad luck," I argued. "And we'll come out somewhere in the middle."

"Wow, '*somewhere in the middle*'!" Zach repeated, his voice dripping with sarcasm. "Just what every student dreams of achieving."

Okay, enough was enough. I'd tried persuasion. I'd

tried encouragement. Now I was desperate, and it was time for my last resort.

"Zach, please." Begging. There's no way Zach could turn me down in my time of greatest need, right? "You're my friend, and I need your help."

"Yeah, um . . ." Zach looked over his shoulder suddenly, as if he'd heard something. "What's that, Coach Pearson?" I followed his gaze, but there was no one there. And there was definitely no one calling his name. Either all this science fair stress was making Zach hallucinate . . . or he was trying to make a fast getaway. "Basketball practice," he said to me confidently, as if he and the imaginary Coach Pearson had just had a brief but crucial conversation. "I'll talk to you later, okay? Like . . . when we're thirty," he finished under his breath.

Zach was up and gone from the table before I could say anything. No matter — he hadn't heard the last of me.

Not by a long shot.

Okay, so I didn't have a plan, not yet. But I did have the lyrics to a new song:

A friend does you a favor.
A friend has got your back.

But if that's true, I'm feeling blue.
What kind of friend is Zach?
And if he really cared,
We'd win the science fair!
Come on, Zach!
Cut me some slack!

You like? I wrote it in study hall that afternoon, and by the time I'd finished, I was totally inspired. I didn't need a sneaky, complicated plan to trick Zach into working with me. I just needed to remind him what it meant to be a best friend. Surely when he remembered all the things I'd done for him, he'd be more than happy to be my partner! Or he'd be miserable to be my partner, but he'd do it, anyway, because I'd stuff him so full of guilt he'd think he was a Thanksgiving turkey.

And I'd start immediately.

First stop: *Juice!*.

Zach stepped up to the counter to get his smoothie. Ben handed him the drink but refused Zach's money.

"This one's on Addie," he explained. He took a closer look at the note I'd slipped him — let's just say Ben's memory usually needs some help. "Uh . . . 'cause you guys are such good fiends!" he read.

24

"*Friends!*" I shouted from my table. Apparently, Ben's memory isn't the only thing that needs help. Zach spotted me in the corner and gave me a feeble smile. It looked to me like an invitation to be science fair partners.

I hopped up from my seat and hurried over to Zach, who was trying his best to pretend I wasn't there. He carried his smoothie over to a table and sat down, spreading his science magazines out and beginning to leaf through them. Guess he still hadn't found a project yet — or a partner. Excellent.

"I was just remembering that time last winter when you forgot your jacket," I said brightly. "And I let you borrow my scarf and hat . . . and I totally caught a cold."

That finally forced Zach to look up at me. He scowled, and looked back down at his magazines.

"That was great, wasn't it?" I asked, ignoring his expression. "Good times."

No response.

"Let me know when you decide about science fair," I added casually. Couldn't hurt, right?

Still silent, Zach rolled his eyes, got up from the table, and walked away from me and out the door.

"Be my science partner!" I shouted after him, desperation making my voice wobble. "Please!"

He didn't even turn around. But that was okay — he could run, but he couldn't hide. Not for long . . .

Take two: Zach's locker, the next morning.

"So, speaking of science fair," I began, once he'd recovered from the shock of seeing me jump out from behind his locker door. "I was thinking that maybe this year —"

"Addie, stop." Zach sighed, and I knew what he was going to say: No. Again. Well, I wasn't going to let him get the words out. He just didn't understand how much I needed him, and how hard I was willing to work. What was it going to take? "I have to tell you something —"

"No, I have to tell *you* something." All the fake bravado leaked out of my voice. I was just honest and told him exactly how much I needed his help. "I know how important winning is to you, and I would never ask you to give that up . . . but I need this for my science grade. So can you help me out? As a friend."

There was a long pause. Zach didn't say anything, but an expression flashed across his face that I couldn't quite read. Then he frowned. Maybe this time, he'd really heard me. Maybe this time, he was ready to help.

He sighed again, then opened his mouth and —

"Zach? Ready?"

I whirled around, and there was Zach's friend Mario, his face lit up by an oblivious grin — he obviously had no idea what he was interrupting. No matter. I turned back to Zach and held my breath, hoping he would still say whatever he'd been about to say.

"Addie . . ." He tried to smile, but it wasn't working. That's when I knew I didn't really want to hear the next words out of his mouth. "I decided to be partners with Mario."

"Oh."

I didn't know what else to say. That was it. The end. I guess I'd always thought that Zach would come through for me. I hadn't let myself think about what would happen if I was wrong. What I would do next.

"It's nothing personal," Zach explained quickly. "I just can't risk being brought down by your jinx."

"I am not jinxed!" I shouted, totally exasperated. Just then, Principal Brandywine sped by us on her motorized scooter, rolling right over my left foot. "Ow!" I squealed in pain, jumping backward.

"Thanks for understanding," Zach mumbled, looking away.

"Did you say something, dear?" Principal Brandywine asked, backing up her scooter so she could hear me better.

I just ignored her — I still couldn't believe what Zach had done. "Understand this!" I yelled in his face. "I am not jinxed!" Then — "*Ow!*" The principal's scooter had rolled over me *again*, in the other direction. For a second, I wondered — was I jinxed? Maybe Zach was right to get as far away from me as he could. Maybe I just brought bad luck down on myself and everyone who was foolish enough to be around me. . . .

But you know what I suddenly realized? That's crazy! There's no way I am jinxed. Like Ms. Gonzalez-Menendez-Mendoza said: There's no such thing as a jinx. And I bet Zach knew that just as well as I did. He was just using the whole jinx thing as an excuse so that he didn't have to feel guilty for ditching me. *Too bad, Zach,* I decided. This year I was going to prove him — and everyone — wrong, once and for all.

"You know what?" I said harshly, ignoring the apologetic look on his face. Sorry wouldn't cut it, not this time. "Just to prove to you that I'm not jinxed, I'm gonna win the science fair this year."

Zach straightened up and looked me defiantly in the eye. "Okay. You do that."

"Well said," Principal Brandywine congratulated us. "It's that kind of competitive spirit that will put Rocky

Road Middle School over the top." She rolled off . . . and rolled over my foot for a third time.

"Aaaaand . . . *ow*," I moaned quietly. After all, I'd almost been expecting it. Maybe I wasn't jinxed — but even I had to admit I was having a pretty unlucky day.

Okay, forget what I said about bad luck. Because only a few hours later, it seemed my day was looking up. Waaaay up. I was sulking in the hallway, throwing stuff into my locker as hard as I could — with each satisfying thump and clatter, I pretended I was chucking books at Zach's head. It made me feel a little better. But not as much as what happened next.

"You are as stubborn as you are crazy!"

I looked up when I heard the girl's loud and angry voice, and there, only a few feet away, Duane Ogilvy and Mary Ferry were having a huge fight. She was bright red and sputtering, and he kept pushing his glasses up on his nose with so much force that I was afraid he might shove them right into his brain.

"I *was* crazy to be science fair partners with you!" Duane shouted back. "Luckily, I've since recovered my faculties."

"Good." Mary Ferry spun away from him, her long

blond braids almost whacking him in the face. She stalked off, pausing only to wish him one last fond farewell over her shoulder: "I hope you and your faculties are very happy together!"

For a second, I stayed very still and very quiet, and tried to keep myself calm. I silently ran through what I'd just heard — had it really happened? Could I have imagined it? Definitely not — but still, it seemed too good to be true. Mary and Duane having a huge fight, right before the science fair? It seemed like one of those crazy fantasies I always have, before I get slammed back into day-to-day bad-luck reality. But this was it — reality — and yet it seemed like things were finally starting to go my way. . . .

Duane slumped over to the outdoor eating area and plopped down at a table. He looked totally dejected. After a few minutes — I didn't want to make it look like I was following him around and making use of his misery, after all, even if it was true — I squeezed into the seat next to him. As best I could, I tried to suppress a grin.

"Looks like you're short a science fair partner," I said casually, as if it didn't matter to me one way or the other.

"Whatever." Duane looked like he was about to cry, but he kept his voice emotionless and steady. "My science grade is high enough. I'm just gonna take the hit."

No! The idea that he might opt out of the science fair hadn't even occurred to me. I *couldn't* let that happen — it would be such a waste of fantastic good luck, for one thing. And for another thing, without Duane's help I would totally fail science.

But I'd tried the honest, begging approach with Zach, and look where that got me. No, this time, I resolved to be a little more . . . subtle.

"That's one way to go," I allowed. "Or . . . you could partner up with someone else — and win. Just to show Mary Ferry how big a mistake she made by leaving you."

Duane looked shocked that I would suggest such a thing — but his surprise passed pretty quick. And soon, it turned into something that looked suspiciously like delight.

"I like your moxie, Singer," he said, nodding and looking impressed. "You're on. Prepare to win the science fair."

I never thought a sentence with the words *science fair* in it could sound so sweet.

Duane and I shook on it — and, just like that, I had myself a science fair partner. And not just any science fair partner — the most brilliant, most ingenious, most science-y guy in the whole school. Zach wouldn't know *what* hit him.

The next afternoon, Ben got home before I did. He strutted through the back door, finding Mom in the kitchen, doing some cleaning.

"What up?" he asked, tossing his basketball from one hand to the other — he's always doing that. He thinks it makes him look cool. Guess what? He's wrong. "I'm home."

Mom cleared off the kitchen counter and carefully set out her new kissing-fish cookie jar. As she did so, Ben missed a catch, and the basketball flew across the room, just missing the jar. "Ben! Be careful with that ball!" Mom cried. "You might . . ." Her voice trailed off, and she got a thoughtful, almost crafty look on her face. ". . . break something."

"Sorry," Ben said, and he stopped tossing the

ball. But anyone who knew Ben would realize that after a couple of minutes, he'd forget and start throwing it around again. And Mom knew Ben the best of anyone. She slid the cookie jar over to the edge of the counter, about a half inch from the end — smiling innocently all the while, as if she just thought it looked best there.

That's when I came in, followed by my fabulous new science fair partner, Duane Ogilvy.

"Hello, Mrs. Singer," Duane greeted Mom, setting down his sack of supplies. "Duane Ogilvy."

Brilliant *and* polite — who could ask for anything more?

"Well, nice to see you again, Duane," Mom said, making a strange face. I could tell she was remembering the last time she'd seen Duane — at my party in the basement, when Duane had been doing an "experiment" to see how many corn dogs he could stuff in his mouth at one time.

"Likewise," Duane said cheerfully. Maybe he didn't notice the strange look — or maybe it was just the same look that most people gave him, so to him, it looked normal. "If you don't mind, Addie and I need to impose our presence on your kitchen."

"Okay," Mom agreed. "Cookie?"

I grabbed one out of the hideously ugly jar, then remembered something.

"Hey, did you get to the surprise at the bottom?" I asked.

Mom wrinkled her nose and leaned toward me. "It's some sort of ceramic worm," she confided in a low voice. "I saw a picture online." She shuddered, as if the ceramic worm had just come to life and crawled up her sleeve. "Gave me nightmares."

"*Ew*," I squealed. Totally gross.

Mom shrugged. "Well, ah . . . it's the thought that counts."

I guess — except what did it say that Dad thought kissing fish and ceramic worms were cute?

Thankfully, I didn't have to put any more thought into that scary question, because it was time to get down to business. Focus. Think: *science fair grand prize*. I was a firm believer in the power of positive thinking — and my thoughts all said that, with Duane by my side, we'd come up with a surefire winning project.

He was pulling out bag after bag of popcorn kernels and laying them on the counter side by side.

"The project. Popcorn. To find the perfect temperature," he explained. "Every kernel cooked, no piece burned."

Okay, I love popcorn as much as the next hungry middle-schooler, but I had to admit, it sounded a little . . . fluffy.

"Are you sure that's good enough to win?" I asked dubiously.

Duane looked up from his popcorn and fixed me with a visionary gaze. "Addie. Imagine ridding the world of that burned popcorn smell. Forever. This baby is in the bag." He heaved a sigh and stared off into space. "Plus . . . Mary Ferry and I had popcorn the first time we went to the movies."

His eyes got all misty, and for a second, I was afraid he was going to cry, but then Duane sucked in a huge breath and forced a smile.

"Okay, over it," he claimed in a choked voice. "Let's pop some corn!"

For the rest of the week, Ms. Gonzalez-Menendez-Mendoza let us work on our projects during science class. And trust me, we *all* needed the extra time.

Zach and Mario had settled on an experiment about reflexes — or maybe I should say that *Zach* had settled on the experiment, and Mario had gone along with him. That's the way their team worked . . . except, it wasn't quite working.

"So . . . let's test those reflexes," Zach said encouragingly. He brandished a little rubber mallet at Mario, who was sitting on the top of a desk with a heating pad on one knee and an ice pack on the other. He didn't look very excited to see the mallet. He looked even less excited when Zach started banging him on the knees with it.

"*Ow*," he yelped, flinching. His right leg bounced up toward Zach, who then hit the other knee. "*Ow!*"

Zach checked his stopwatch, then made some notes in his lab book.

"Okay, let's go again," he suggested, "with two minutes of heat and cold."

Mario winced at the thought of it. "Dude, I gotta take a break."

Zach looked up from his notebook and frowned. "Marlo," he said sternly, shaking his head, "it's like Randy Klein always says — winners don't take breaks."

Mario grimaced and hopped off the table. "Well, winners must have bigger bladders than me." And he walked away.

And they weren't the only ones having problems. Geena and Julian were over on the other side of the room, still hard at work on their artistic masterpiece. They'd put together this spectacular poster covered with velvet, glitter, and a bunch of random scientific words. Geena was trying to figure out the right color for the trim.

"Complementing colors might soothe the judges' tired eyes," she mused, almost to herself, "but contrasting tones would give us the extra attention we need."

"Geena," Julian mumbled. He wasn't a big fan of talking clearly. Or — under normal circumstances — talking at all. But these weren't normal circumstances. This was science fair. "What's our actual *project* going to be?"

Geena flipped her hair back and fixed Julian with a disdainful stare. "Julian, you just concentrate on using your superior art skills to make it pretty," she commanded him. "Leave the rest up to me."

"I don't do pretty," Julian protested. "I do interesting. Unusual. Art."

But Geena wasn't paying attention. She was too busy wondering whether a pink fur trim would make their poster seem unprofessional . . . or irresistible.

And of course, this leads us to my least favorite science fair team, Jake Behari and Patti Perez. Well, Jake Behari isn't my least favorite anything — but every time I saw him paired up with Patti, I wanted to throw up. I mean, he's just so . . . and she's so . . .

Um, where was I?

Oh, right, science fair.

Anyway . . . Jake and Patti were tending to their little patches of grass. Actually, Jake was tending. Patti was on her cell phone, getting the latest gossip download from one of her airhead friends.

"So, the crabgrass with a third cup of water a day seems to be the best combination," Jake reported, examining the brownish stalks in one of his grass patches. "Can you make the notation?"

"Uh-huh," Patti mumbled. "He did not. He did *not!*"

Jake looked up in confusion — and quickly realized that Patti was totally ignoring him in favor of whoever she was on the phone with.

"I'm gonna get some air," Jake muttered.

Patti just held up a finger to shush him, pointing to the phone, as if to silently say, *I'm* talking *here — could you be any ruder?*

"No, go ahead," she said into the phone. "It was just stupid science fair junk." There was a pause, then she raised her eyebrows in disbelief. "He did not. He did *not!*"

Jake shook his head and walked out of the room. I wished I could go with him. As a matter of fact, I would have been happy to go anywhere, as long as it was away from Duane Ogilvy. I thought I'd made a brilliant choice, picking a science fair partner who was smarter than everyone else in our class. But I hadn't realized just how bummed out Duane was — and after a few days of listening to him talk about Mary Ferry, I was going crazy.

"Duane! Concentrate!" I yelled as the pot of popcorn exploded in his face.

"I can't." Duane sighed and pushed himself away from the table. "Everything I know about chemistry, I learned from Mary Ferry." And then, as if he couldn't even say her name without seeking her out, Duane called out to her as she walked past us.

"Hey, Addie and I are sure having fun doing science fair together," he boasted. Fun? That was news to me.

"Oh, *really?*" Mary Ferry replied, pretending she couldn't care less. "Maybe you should marry her."

"Maybe I will," Duane snapped.

"Maybe you should."

"Maybe I will."

"Maybe you should."

"Maybe I will."

"Maybe you should."

And they kept going. And going. And —

And then I stopped paying attention, because suddenly Jake Behari had come back into the room — and was standing right in front of me.

"Science fair," he said, shaking his head and gesturing around us, as if to say that those two words could sum up all the craziness in the world.

"I know," I agreed. Usually when Jake is around, I'm totally tongue-tied. But after forty-two minutes in a row of hearing Duane tell me everything there was to know about Mary Ferry, I was too tired to be nervous. I was just desperate for some normal conversation with a normal human being. And it didn't hurt that this human being was incredibly cute! "I have to win," I explained, "'cause if Zach wins, then he was right about not choosing me, but I have to be right, you know?"

"I'm just trying to pass," Jake said, and for some reason I got the sense that he hadn't even heard me. He seemed a little lost in his own head. "But Patti couldn't care less. I think I picked the wrong partner, you know?"

"Yeah. I do."

But I didn't, not really. I mean, obviously he was sorry he'd partnered up with Patti. But why was he telling me? Did he mean that he wished he had picked me instead? Was that possible? Or was I just the first person he saw on his way back into the room? Why was this science fair stuff so confusing!

"Maybe next time," Jake said, staring intently at me, "I'll pick more carefully."

What did *that* mean? But before I could try to find out, Zach bounded up and interrupted us. And he didn't even notice.

"Addie! We need to talk!"

Jake slipped away before I could stop him, so I shrugged my shoulders and gave Zach my full attention. Not that he deserved it, after the way he'd ditched me for Mario.

"What do you want?" I asked irritably.

"About the whole science fair partner thing . . ."

Was he actually going to apologize? Finally? Beg me to work with him? Tell me that my so-called jinx didn't matter nearly as much as our friendship?

"I want Duane," Zach confessed.

Funny, that didn't sound like an apology to me.

"You should give him up," Zach explained, "so he and I can be partners. For the good of the school."

"What?!"

"Addie, if I have Duane on my side, I can win. I just need a little help."

"Oh, now *you* need a little help?" I asked incredulously. I could feel my face getting red, the way it does when I get really, really angry. Zach must be totally desperate if he'd fooled himself into thinking I could go for this. "Where were you when *I* needed a little help?"

"Please, you need a *lot* of help," Zach retorted.

I don't know what I would have done next if Geena hadn't stepped in between us and pushed us apart — but I suspect Zach might have ended up with a fistful of popcorn mashed in his face.

"Whoa, whoa, whoa, break it up," Geena urged us, playing peacemaker. "It's just science fair. Now, come on. What we need is a nice afternoon away from all this stuff. The three of us are going to *Juice!*. And no one's going to talk about science. Got it?"

Geena looked at me, I looked at Zach, and Zach looked up at the ceiling. We both shrugged at exactly the same moment. And I knew we were thinking the same thing — there would be no cease-fire, no truce. Not until the science fair — not until someone won. And someone else apologized.

Guess which "someone" I was going to be?

In case you were wondering about Mom and her battle with the ugliest cookie jar in the world, they were

43

both still in one piece — which was driving Mom crazy. One day, just before Ben came home, she set the cookie jar on the edge of the kitchen counter, and waited for the inevitable. After a few minutes, Ben slammed through the back door and, like he always does, flung his backpack off his shoulder and onto the counter. It skidded past the cookie jar, and the kissing fish rocked gently back and forth. Mom held her breath as the jar wobbled back and forth, back and forth, and seemed ready to tip over the edge and crash to the ground, breaking into a million pieces. . . .

But it didn't.

On another day, she might have stopped there, given up. But she was frustrated, thwarted — and tired of looking at that fish's kissy face every time she walked into the kitchen. So she picked up Ben's backpack and, slowly, steadily, approached the cookie jar. If she threw it herself, if she aimed for the jar, she knew she couldn't miss. And no one would ever be able to prove it hadn't been an accident —

And that's when my dad walked through the door.

Busted!

Mom dropped the backpack and grinned guiltily at my father.

He didn't notice a thing.

We now return you to our regularly scheduled pro-gramming — my jinxed life. When last we checked, Zach and I were facing off, while Geena tried to calm us down. Hours later and miles away, nothing much had changed.

Geena had convinced us to come to *Juice!* together, as if nothing had happened, but I was refusing to pre-tend that I wasn't mad at Zach. And it looked like he felt the same way.

"So . . ." Geena had been chattering nonstop since we walked in the door, maybe thinking that if she talked enough, we wouldn't notice that she was talking to her-self. "Did you notice Mr. Ward's hair today? It didn't move at all, even when he bent down to pick up that eraser. I totally think it's a toupee."

Silence, as Zach and I glared at each other.

"This is the good gossip here, guys," Geena pointed out. "I'm pulling out all the stops."

Fortunately, we were saved from any further efforts to have a good time when a group of St. Agnes girls pranced over to our table. They were wearing match-ing white collared shirts and plaid dresses.

"Oh, hi, Zach," the one in the middle said, wearing an obviously fake smile. "I hear you're the favorite to go to regionals this year."

"Got that right," Zach confirmed.

"Jolene and I can't wait to see you there and kick your butt," one of the other girls said cheerfully.

I couldn't take it anymore. Now perfect strangers were coming up to us and acting like Zach was this big famous science fair guy? Like it was already decided that he was going to win? That he was going to beat *me?* No way — not this year.

"For your information, Zach won't be going to regionals this year," I informed the St. Agnes girls. "So you won't be kicking his butt. You'll be kicking mine."

"Perfect," the first girl chirped, flashing me a smile. "See ya then!"

They burst into giggles and walked away, as I went over the conversation in my head and realized what I'd just said.

"Wait . . ." I protested. "That didn't come out right."

But the girls were already gone — and Zach and Geena were laughing too hard to hear me.

"It's been fun," Zach said, smirking, once he'd finally calmed himself down. "But I gotta get back to work." He gulped down the rest of his smoothie and stood up. "That's what winners do."

"How would you know?!" I shouted after him — but

Zach was already gone, and the only one to react was Geena.

"Um — *ow*," she said pointedly, shrinking away. I'd shouted in her ear. Oops.

"I'm sorry. He's just so..." How could I explain the way Zach and his stupid, smirky, jerky attitude got under my skin? There were no words. "*Arghhhhhhh!*" I finally yelled in frustration.

Geena gave me a dirty look and covered her ears.

Like I said — oops.

That night, I was so upset about the whole science fair thing that I couldn't sleep. Okay, so I was mad at Zach — but he was still one of my best friends, and I hated the way things were between us. If only there were an easy way to fix things. I tossed and turned, going over and over all our fights in my head. I couldn't stop hearing his voice telling me I was jinxed when it came to science fair. And you know, maybe I was — after all, the science fair hadn't even happened yet, and already it had messed everything up.

Finally, I gave up on sleep. I flicked on my light, sat up in bed, and grabbed my guitar. Just like I always do when I'm upset.

Like a bad science fair volcano, everything just blew up.

The experiment we call friendship has somehow run amok.

How did things get so messed up?

How did I lose a friend?

I wanna win the science fair — but is it worth it in the end?

Was winning worth destroying a friendship?

I didn't know — and I was afraid to find out.

Ben blew through the kitchen door after a hard shift at *Juice!*. He slapped his basketball down on the kitchen counter — coming within an inch of knocking the kissing-fish cookie jar to the floor.

"Of all the fruits," he mused, "papaya is the hardest one to juice. All those seeds!" Ever since Ben started working at *Juice!*, he's picked up all these bits of fruit "wisdom" — and he just loves sharing them. That's when Ben noticed how close he'd come to kicking the cookie jar. He picked it up carefully and moved it toward the center of the counter.

"Mom, you gotta be more careful of that thing," he chided her. "I almost broke it."

Mom wandered into the living room, plopped down on the couch, flopped her head back, and sighed.

"I give up."

Ben threw himself into the easy chair next to her and swung around to look at her, the truth finally sinking in.

"You were *trying* to break it, weren't you?" he asked in disbelief.

"No. Absolutely not." Mom chewed on the bottom of her lip, and looked away. "I'll give you ten bucks to accidentally knock it over," she said softly. "No questions asked."

"Mom, isn't that kinda childish?" Ben pointed out. "If you don't like it, just tell Dad."

"You're right," Mom admitted. "I should just tell him the truth." She kicked her feet up on the table next to Ben's chair as she continued, "Besides, it's the thought that —" There was a long and loud crash, as her feet knocked over a lamp...which knocked Ben's ball out of his hands...and sent it flying across the room, straight into the fan... which spun around and blew over a book...which sent the cookie jar toppling off the table and onto the floor. Where it shattered into a pile of ugly porcelain pieces.

"That was an accident," Mom claimed, stunned. "I swear."

Ben smiled knowingly and patted her on the shoulder. "Hey, whatever you have to tell yourself to sleep at night."

Mom ignored Ben and hurried to get a broom and dustpan so that she could get rid of the incriminating evidence. She was fast . . . but not fast enough.

"Hey, what happened?" Dad asked, walking through the door to discover his gift in a pile on the floor.

"Oh, honey, it broke," Mom confessed sadly. "I'm so sorry."

"Before you got to the surprise?"

Mom put a gentle hand on his shoulder and nodded.

"Yeah, sweetie, about the surprise . . ." She took a deep breath. Honesty may be the best policy, but it's almost never the easy one. "I saw the little worm online. And it's cute, I suppose, but . . ."

As she was talking, Dad reached into the trash bag and fished around for the little ceramic worm.

"Truth is," Mom continued, cringing when she saw what he was doing, "I was only looking at that cookie jar online because it was so ugly, and I'm sorry I didn't say anything, but . . . but . . ."

Before she could think of something to say that would be honest and tactful at the same time, she noticed something about the little ceramic worm that Dad had handed her. It was as ugly as it had looked online — but there was something different about it. The ugly little worm was holding a beautiful diamond bracelet in its mouth.

Mom looked up at Dad in confusion, then threw her arms around him. Dad folded her into a tight embrace, grinning.

"I told you there was a surprise at the bottom," he said sweetly.

Parents can get really mushy sometimes.

It felt like we'd been waiting forever — but the day was finally here. The day that I would finally prove to myself and the world that I wasn't jinxed, that I had just as much chance of winning the science fair as any other kid. In fact, with Duane by my side, I had the best chance of anyone in the room.

"This is it," Duane intoned as he set up our hot plate and carefully poured a cup of popcorn kernels into our nonstick pan (courtesy of my mom). "Today we will make science fair history."

I was only half listening to him, because I was busy surveying the competition. It looked pretty stiff — but I wasn't afraid. I was ready.

"Zach and Mary Ferry are gonna be sorry when we kick their science fair butts and rub our victory in their faces," I said defiantly, trying to psych myself up.

"That's terrible," Duane gasped. He shook his head and gave me the same look that our history teacher gave Geena when she wanted to write her term paper on the history of shopping. "Science fair should be shared with someone special," Duane said sadly. "It's not about winning or losing. It's about learning — advancing the study of the universe. I've been a fool."

"Yeah, but . . . we're still gonna win, right?"

Geena and Julian were still putting the finishing touches on their project. Or should I say, their poster. Because basically, that's all there was.

"It *is* beautiful," Geena gushed, gazing at the poster. It was painted a deep, dark blue and covered with glittering stars. "Julian, we're geniuses."

"Geena, they're gonna figure out that there's no project here," Julian argued.

"Isn't there?"

Julian looked at her questioningly, but Geena just smiled in that mysterious way she has, and stayed silent as the judges approached.

"Geena. Julian. This is a lovely display," Ms. Gonzales-Menendez-Mendoza finally said, after search-ing their poster for some evidence of an actual science project. She couldn't find any. "But . . ."

"Caught your eye, didn't it?" Geena asked quickly. "You see, our project this year is just that. We're doing a study on flash over substance. Using the other, more typical projects as our control group."

Julian smiled as he caught on to what she was doing.

"We're comparing our ability to attract judges based entirely on lights, flashy lettering, and fake fur," he explained. (That may be the most words Julian has ever said at one time.)

And you know what the strangest thing was?

The judges bought it.

Over at Mario and Zach's table, things were a little less . . . friendly.

They had set up a tall screen for Mario to sit behind, so that only his legs would stick out.

"So then, we'll show them a demonstration, and the rest will be history," Zach explained. For the tenth time.

"Zach, I know," Mario complained.

"And you should let me do most of the talking," Zach continued.

"Zach, I know."

"And make sure to always smile and —"

"Zach! They won't even be able to see my face!" Mario exploded.

Zach smiled patronizingly and adopted a patient tone, as if he were a teacher talking to an especially slow student. "But Randy Klein always says, a smile will go a million miles —"

"That's enough, man," Mario interrupted. "I'm not Randy Klein! I'm not." He stormed away, stopping a few feet away as something else occurred to him that he had to get off his chest. "And how come I always have to be the one getting his knees pounded on?"

"Okay, we set the hot plate for exactly thirty seconds," Duane reminded me as the judges stopped to look at a project a few tables away from us. The closer they got, the louder my heart pounded — whatever happened in the next twenty minutes would decide my science fair fate — not to mention my grade in science. "But we have to watch closely or —"

But Duane wasn't even watching it himself anymore — his voice trailed off as he spotted Mary Ferry approaching. It looked like she was going to pass right by us, but then, as if attracted by some kind of magnetic pull, she drifted closer and closer, until she was standing right in front of Duane. They stared at each other for a long, tense moment, not saying anything.

"Nice project," Mary Ferry finally commented.

"I did it all for you," Duane admitted. "You know, 'cause we had popcorn —"

"When we went to the movies!" Mary Ferry finished with him. You could tell she was touched by the gesture.

"I'm so sorry we were fighting," Duane said in a choked voice. Part of me wanted to roll my eyes . . . but the other part of me was almost ready to cry. It was so obvious how much they liked each other, and how upset they'd been about not speaking to each other. And I could feel their pain. After all, Zach and I hadn't talked in days, and it was killing me to be in such a huge fight with such a good friend.

"I'm so sorry we were fighting," Duane told her again.

"No, I'm sorry," Mary Ferry protested. "I don't even remember what it was about."

"Oh, I do. You said the moon landing was faked in Burbank, which is such a ridiculous conspiracy theory that —" he stopped himself suddenly, gulped, and with a pained look on his face, finished — "it must be right."

Mary Ferry beamed at him.

Okay, so at that point I *did* roll my eyes. I couldn't help it. But I also couldn't help being a little jealous. Duane and Mary Ferry were so happy — and every time I looked across the room at Zach and thought about our fight, I was totally miserable. Much as I hated to admit it, all the science fair trophies in the world wouldn't fix that.

Zach had looked for Mario everywhere, but he was nowhere to be found. Which left Zach with nothing to say when the judges finally got to his table. He stood in front of his screen, searching for a way to explain that the subject of his experiment had gone missing.

"So, um, I was going to demonstrate the results, but . . ."

I wish I could have seen the look on his face when he noticed a pair of legs sliding out from beneath the screen. But I couldn't see him, of course, because I was behind the screen. Where else would a best friend be?

"But . . . I'll go ahead and do it now," Zach babbled, thinking fast. "First . . ." He grabbed his rubber mallet. "The average reflex before heat or cold is applied."

He hit me on the knee, and the next thing I knew,

my leg was bouncing up — and I felt my foot hit something with a soft thud.

"*Oof*," Zach said loudly. "Strong reflexes."

There was some chattering from the judges, and
then Zach — doubled over and clutching his stomach —
pulled away the curtain. The judges were gone.

"Oops," I said, trying to cover up my smile.
"Sorry."

Zach shrugged. "You tried," he pointed out.
"Thanks."

I hopped off the table and came out from behind
the curtain — just in time to see the judges approaching
my own project. In my hurry to rescue Zach, I'd almost
forgotten about the popcorn heating up on our table.
And I guess Duane had forgotten about it, too, because I
couldn't see him anywhere.

"Uh, I gotta go before —"

Too late.

The popcorn exploded all over the place, right in
the judges' faces. Hmm . . . wonder if they'd believe me
if I told them that the goal of our project had been to
simulate a blizzard — with popcorn.

Probably not.

"Jinxed again." I sighed.

Zach won't partner with Addie because he is determined to win — maybe a little too determined. . . .

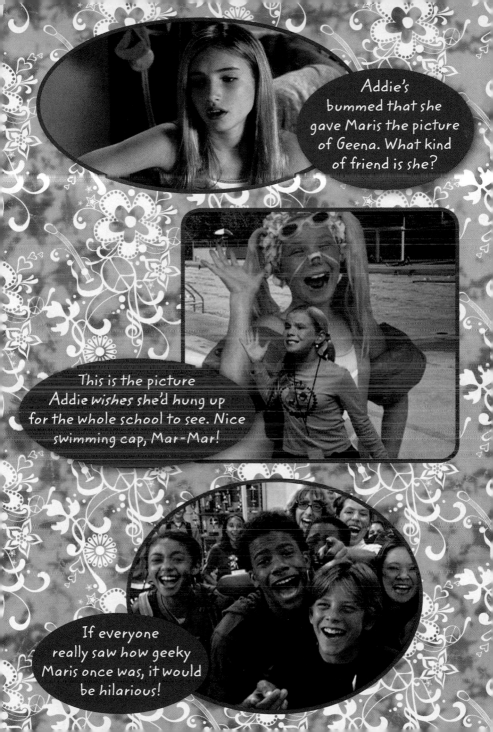

My nose is stuffy. My eyes are puffy. Snot is in my head. Oh, how I wish that I was dead. It's what I deserve for being a jerk. Every painful sneeze and every gross dry heave . . .

Addie's real friends come through for her in the end.

And they bring her magazines and soup to make her feel better. Geena and Zach are totally the best!

Zach patted me on the back with a weary grin. "Nah. We'll get it right next year."

We?

"Science fair isn't only about the win," Zach said, sounding like he meant it. "Sorry I got so wrapped up in it."

I shrugged. After all, Zach wasn't the only one to blame — I'd gotten pretty wrapped up in it, too. I was just glad things were getting back to normal. Well, almost normal.

I pointed toward Mario, who was sitting against the wall with the school nurse hovering over him. He had bags of ice covering both his knees.

"Actually," I reminded Zach, "there's someone else you should probably apologize to."

Zach made it to science fair regionals, as usual. He even agreed to let Mario pound on his knees. Unfortunately, he didn't win.

As if we needed a reminder, the next day at *Juice!*, we ran into the St. Agnes girls — and they had brought along their giant trophy.

"Good work, science fair girls," the one with the long blond hair cheered. "Yay for us!"

"I can see my reflection in the cup," one of her teammates marveled, checking to make sure she didn't have anything in her teeth.

"Let's fill this with juice and order three straws," the other teammate suggested, bursting into giggles.

Over at our table, Zach and I rolled our eyes at the very same instant. That's how you knew things were really back to normal.

"Sorry about regionals," I told him, not for the first time.

"Eh." He shrugged. "Geena was right. We should've worn matching plaid vests."

"And bow ties," I added, choking on my laughter.

"And argyle socks," Geena spit out through her giggles.

And that's how the three of us laughed the afternoon away, until the whole science fair saga was completely forgotten. If you're really friends with someone, you can repair the little cracks. And you never even see the seams where it was broken.

At least, that's what Mom told me after she finally managed to glue all the pieces of the kissing-fish cookie jar back together, as a special present for Dad. She wanted him to know how much it meant to her, ugly or not. She put it out on the counter for him to see, and waited for him to get home and see what she'd done.

"Hey, honey, I'm home," he said, as he walked through the door and tossed his bag on the counter. In exactly the wrong place.

CRASH!

Mom and Dad exchanged a glance as the repaired cookie jar smashed onto the floor. Then they burst into laughter together.

Well, I still believe friendships can always be repaired if you try hard enough. But I guess cookie jars are another story.

You'd think that once the science fair was over everything got back to normal. And it did — for a while. But that's the thing about middle school. Just when you think your week is going to be nice and normal, something totally unexpected happens and throws everything out of whack. That "something" can come from anywhere — a new kid in school, a new option in the cafeteria, a new stain that suddenly appears right in the middle of your brand-new shirt — *anywhere*. It's a dangerous world out there. So I guess I shouldn't have been surprised last week when one of those "somethings" happened again. But I was. It caught me completely off guard. And it almost ruined everything.

Before I start, I should explain something about myself — I would do anything for my two best friends, Geena and Zach. And they would do anything for me.

I know, I know, the whole science fair thing was a little confusing, but every friendship hits some bumps in the road. In the end, the science fair just made the three of us better friends than ever. Some people might say we don't have that much in common — and they'd be right. We're totally different from one another. But you know what? That's what I love the most about us.

I mean, why is it that some people only like hanging out with people who are exactly like them? I don't know how it is in your school, but in my school, the jocks hang out with the jocks, the artists hang out with the artists, and the geeks hang out with the geeks. And I guess it goes without saying that the popular kids won't talk to anyone but one another. I guess they've got plenty of stuff to talk about, but personally, I think that would get super boring after a while.

Like I say, Geena, Zach, and I are totally different from one another. But that's what makes it interesting. Take last Monday, for example, when we met at our lockers for the standard download of our weekend adventures.

"This weekend was awesome," Zach said. "I spent Saturday gathering petition signatures to create a moth sanctuary in Kingston Park."

"Aren't moths just ugly butterflies?" Geena asked, wrinkling her nose.

"They're the most intelligent of the winged insects!" Zach countered angrily. "Ignorance like that is why I only got nine signatures!"

I'm not saying we don't argue — but that's kind of the beauty of it. We always have stuff to talk about, and we always have fun. Yes, we have different points of view on almost everything. But that means learning something new about the world — or each other — almost every day. I'd way rather be friends with them than some cookie-cutter clones.

"Hey, guys!" I said loudly, trying to interrupt their bickering. "Geena, don't forget this Saturday, we're going to the grand opening —"

"— of L.G.E.," Geena finished with me. "Lip Gloss Emporium. I've had it marked on my calendar for months."

"You know what else is this Saturday?" Zach asked. Geena and I leaned in eagerly, hoping we'd hear about some supercool activity we could check out after stocking up on lip gloss. "The sweatshop workers who made that lip gloss are having a parade to celebrate the three cents an hour they were paid."

"Really?" Geena asked. "We better leave early, then. We don't want to get stuck in parade traffic."

Zach started to respond, but Geena elbowed him and gave him a teasing grin, just to let him know she was joking. We all laughed and walked down the hall together. See what I mean? We were all happy together. Everything was nice and normal.

That was Monday morning. But by Friday, everything had changed.

Want a sneak preview? Fast-forward just a few days, and you'd see Geena and me in exactly the same hallway. Except that Geena was with Cranberry St. Claire, of all people, wheeling a slide projector down the hall. And I was standing with Maris Bingham — one of the only girls in school who's just as snotty and popular as Cranberry — facing them down.

"Excuse me, Blond and Blonder?" Geena snapped. "Your giant egos are in our way."

I rolled my eyes at Maris, then spoke slowly and clearly, as if Geena didn't speak English.

"I'm sorry, *no comprendo.* We. Don't. Speak. Geek."

Maris and I touched wiggling fingers and cried out together, "Burn!" Then we laughed in their faces and, in sync, whirled around and strutted away down the hall.

No, it wasn't Geena's nightmare. It was mine. Except I was awake — and it was for real.

I guess I should back up a little. As usual, I blame Mr. Ward, our social studies teacher.

It was first thing Monday morning, and we were sitting in class, listening to Mr. Ward give us a long speech about something we already knew too much about: the brutal, dog-eat-dog world also known as middle-school social life.

"Jocks. Populars. AV Geeks. Burnouts. Wannabes," Mr. Ward said, pacing slowly through the classroom. "They're all labels. Cliques. Reps. Words used to divide the student body into a social hierarchy."

Okay . . . so tell me something I don't know.

"Wouldn't it be a better world if people of all shapes, sizes, and social standing could be friends?" Mr. Ward continued. "If nerds and popular kids could hold hands?"

Duane Ogilvy must have forgotten himself in the spirit of the moment, because he suddenly got inspired to reach over and grab Maris's hand.

"Huzzah!" he cried, holding it up in the air.

Maris yanked her hand away with a squeal and held it out toward Cranberry.

"*Ew*. It held my hand," she complained, starting to freak out. "Disinfect."

Cranberry dug through her purse and pulled out a small bottle of disinfectant, squirting a blob of it on Maris's outstretched hand. Mr. Ward did his best to ignore her. It seemed like a pretty good idea to me.

"*So*," he said pointedly, picking up a box of ID tags from his desk, "here's your assignment. I'm going to give each of you a social label. For the next week, you must hang out only with the other people who are in your designated clique."

The class groaned in unison, just like we always do when Mr. Ward hands out one of his "creative" assignments. Here's the thing he doesn't seem to realize: They almost always end in complete disaster.

"Let's take a walk in the other guy's shoes, shall we?" he asked, ignoring our groans. He reached into his box and started pulling out ID tags, handing them to kids as he walked up and down the rows of desks.

"Artsy — Nick," he said, handing the tag to the video game freak sitting in front of Zach. "Jock — Brianna." That one went to the girl behind Zach. "Popular — Maris."

"Of course," Maris said with snotty delight, placing the tag around her neck.

"Future CEO of America?" Mr. Ward looked around the classroom and, with a slow smile, handed the ID tag to Zach.

"Wait!" Zach yelped. "An FCEO of A? So for a week I have to be a corporate clone? A suit? The *man?*"

But Mr. Ward didn't seem to care about Zach's dismay. He'd already moved on to wreaking havoc in someone else's life.

"AV Geek . . . Geena."

"I don't know what that is," Geena protested.

But I didn't have time to worry about Geena, because Mr. Ward was coming closer and closer to my desk. What would he pull out of his box for me? I wondered. It would decide my fate for the rest of the week — and based on my history with school projects (the word *jinxed* comes to mind), it didn't seem like the news would be good.

"Popular," Mr. Ward continued. "Addie."

Popular? Me?

Cranberry seemed even more taken aback than I was.

"Yeah, right!" she laughed meanly. "Why don't you just take the F now?"

I was about to say something smart and bitter back — at least, I was trying to think of something — when

Mr. Ward handed Cranberry an ID tag of her own: AV Geek.

"What is this?" she gasped. "Some kind of joke?"

Newsflash, Cranberry: You are now officially an Audiovisual Geek. I guess you'll be setting up Mr. Ward's next slide show. I'd think it was hilarious if I didn't have my own problems to worry about.

The class was almost over, so Mr. Ward hurried back to the front of the room to give us the week's rules.

"Once you step outside the classroom, you will live as your label for the rest of the week. Cheating will result in points off your final grade," he warned. "Obviously, I can't be everywhere, so Eli will act as my eyes and ears."

Eli Pataki had plenty of practice at that kind of thing, since his unofficial job was to spy on the student population for Principal Brandywine. Tattling on people was his favorite hobby, and we all knew that he'd be eager to tell Mr. Ward if he caught any of us cheating.

"Be afraid," Eli threatened us. "Be very afraid."

The bell rang, and the class started to gather our stuff, already buzzing about Mr. Ward's weird project.

Zach slipped his ID tag around his neck with a sigh. "Well, I guess this is the chance to see what makes those soulless, no-conscience, 'hey, let's all mess up the planet' jerks tick."

That's the spirit, Zach.

"Okay, Ms. Popular," Geena teased me, "don't let your new rep go to your head."

"Please. It's just a dumb assignment," I reminded them. "I'll meet you guys at the lockers at lunch."

That's when Eli popped up between us. I don't know how that kid manages to be everywhere at once. It's a special talent. And a *really* irritating one.

"I don't think so," Eli said triumphantly. "Future CEOs, AV Geeks, and Populars do *not* eat lunch together." He waved a pad of pink slips in our faces. "I'd hate to have to report you to Mr. Ward."

The three of us turned to glare at him, and he backed away. But before he went out the door, he pointed to his eyes, then to us, and his message was clear: "I'm watching you." Great. Just great.

Geena shrugged. "Oh, well," she said as cheerfully as she could. "Let's get this stupid assignment over with. I'm off to turn AV Geek into AV Chic!"

As we walked out of the room, I tried not to giggle at the sight of Cranberry St. Claire slumped over her desk, weeping at the thought of spending even a minute in geekdom.

"It's okay, Cranberry," Mr. Ward said in a comforting tone. "It's just for a week." He handed her a stack of DVDs. "Here. I think you'll find these helpful. It's all seventy-four episodes of *Star Trek*."

Ben wasn't having the best of days, either. It was the middle of the day, but he was all done with school — one of the perks of being struck down by the dreaded flu. Sick days always sound so good in theory: lying around in bed, watching TV and drinking orange juice while Mom waits on you hand and foot. . . . There's just one problem when you've got the flu, you're too miserable to enjoy any of it.

"Thanks for picking me up from school, Mom," Ben wheezed as he shuffled through the back door. "I don't know what happened. I think Rick Neederhorn coughed on my burrito at lunch and —" He was overtaken by a sneezing fit before he could continue.

"Aw, Benjie," Mom said, using the nickname Ben always claimed to despise. He'd been Benjie until he was about twelve — then he'd suddenly gotten too "cool" for it. But he was too sick to hate anything right now. "Why don't you curl up on the couch and I'll bring you some soup?"

Ben gazed up at Mom with wide, pitiful eyes.

"Chicken with stars and alphabets?" he sniffled hopefully.

"Of course." She ruffled Ben's hair, which is something else he usually thinks he's too cool for these days.

"Make sure all the letters are there," Ben reminded her feebly.

"'Cause it's not the same if you can't spell your name," they continued together, laughing at the familiar motto.

Ben walked slowly toward the couch and eased himself down with a soft groan. Mom covered him with a blanket, then hurried off to the kitchen to start heating up his soup. I'm sure she felt bad for Ben and all — but still, you couldn't help but notice that she was suppressing a little smile.

"I love it when they get sick," she mumbled to herself. Mom loves being needed and able to baby Ben.

Back at school, Zach was getting his first lesson in Corporate America 101. He was stuck at a table with the Future CEOs of America — and when I say "stuck," I mean he stuck out like a sore thumb. The rest of them were all wearing these totally preppy suits and ties, like they thought Rocky Road Middle School was just their first step toward corporate greatness. Zach, on the other hand, was wearing a ratty green T-shirt that he'd explained just that morning had been made out of environmentally friendly corn silk, with all proceeds going to support the national Save the Mosquitoes campaign. It was going to be an *interesting* meal.

"What's more important than money?" asked Chip, the unofficial leader of the FCEOs of A. He was trying to give the new members a crash course in business smarts.

"Uh, everything?" Zach guessed.

"Close," Chip allowed. "*Nothing*. Earning money is our number one priority. After all, in the twenty-first century, a billion is the new million."

"Wow," Zach gasped. "With a billion dollars, I could save the rain forests . . . and the whales!"

"Uh-huh, uh-huh," Chip muttered, his eyes glazing over as he dreamed of the financial possibilities. "I like it. Untapped marketing resource. But how would we get our logo to stay on the back of a whale?"

Uh . . . perhaps it's best if we move on before we see Zach's reaction. Let's just say it wasn't pretty.

Anyway, over at my table, I was drowning in perkiness, as a bunch of popular-girl wannabes struggled to get Maris's stamp of approval.

". . . And then my sister was all, you're out!" this

one über-perky girl was saying, maybe thinking that if she talked fast enough, Maris wouldn't remember that the only reason we were all sitting together was because of a school project. "And I was, like, 'Nu-uh, I totally did not get tagged.' And I hadn't, 'cause I was touching home base. Does 'oly-oly-oxen-free' mean *nothing* anymore?"

Uh, okay. I'm not saying that *I'm* cool or anything, but even I know that hide-and-seek cafeteria chat went out in the fifth grade. As a reflex, I looked over to roll my eyes at Geena ... but of course, Geena wasn't sitting there anymore. Thanks to Mr. Ward's dumb project, Geena was stuck at the AV Geek table, and I was looking straight at Maris. Oops.

Maris, who'd been gazing off into space, looking bored out of her mind, suddenly sat up straight and nodded at Perky Girl.

"You. Put a sock in it." Then, just as abruptly, she turned toward me. "You. Come with me." Without waiting to see if I would listen to her, she got up and walked away. I guess Maris is used to giving people orders.

And ... I don't know, maybe I was in the mood to follow them. Because that's just what I did.

"Look, I can't take this for a whole week," Maris explained, when I caught up with her. "Lunch is a very

74

important meal for my digestive well-being. I need someone I can hang out with for real."

And that applied to me how? Surely she couldn't
mean —

"*Me?*" I burst into laughter as her words sank in.
"Are you crazy? Why would I want to hang out with you?"

"Oh, I'll show you why."

I couldn't imagine what Maris thought would convince me to forget all those years she'd been mean to
me, ignored me, made fun of me — why in the world
would I want to do anything that would make her life
easier? Why would I want to voluntarily *spend time* with
her? Yuck.

But still, I followed her down the hallway and
stood patiently behind her as she opened her locker. The
locker door seemed to fold back on itself like a fan. This
wasn't your average locker . . . it was huge . . . it was . . .
And then she opened the one next to it.

"You have *two* lockers?" I asked incredulously.
Until this year, I only had half of one!

"Courtesy of the sixth-grade nerds," Maris
explained with a shrug, as if it should have been obvious. "Nerds have been donating their lockers to popular
kids forever. Why do you think their backpacks are
always so big?"

Huh. I guess I'd never really thought of it before. She pointed out a couple of nerds walking by us down the hall, pulling their massive backpacks on wheels.

"Hi, Maris!" one called. "How's your locker? I'm having a party on —"

"No," Maris snapped.

"Did you hear that, Edmond?" the nerd gushed to his friend. "She just talked to me!"

"Sweet," I murmured, peeking my head into her giant locker — she'd managed to knock down the division between the two, and now had a cavernous space for storing all her stuff.

I guess I should have been totally disgusted and repulsed by it all. But I wasn't.

I couldn't help it.

I was impressed.

Being popular definitely had its perks.

I took a furtive glance over my shoulder. The coast was clear.

"Hey," I whispered.

· Geena slid her quarter into the soda machine and refused to look at me.

"The *walls* have *ears*," she whispered back meaningfully.

"Huh?"

Just then, Eli Pataki slipped out from his hiding place, and I figured it out.

"I didn't just hear a Popular talking to an AV Geek, did I?" he asked, a weaselly grin lighting up his face. "I'd *hate* to have to report you."

"I'd hate to have to shake this root beer really hard and spray you in the face," Geena retorted, shaking the can at him. But we all knew that it was an empty threat. As long as Eli had that little pink pad, and as long as he had Mr. Ward's ear, we were sunk. She shrugged in my direction and walked away. So much for hanging out with a real friend.

Lucky for me, my fake one had just arrived.

"What are you doing?" Maris asked in horror as I pulled out a couple of quarters to slip into the vending machine.

"Getting a soda," I pointed out. Duh.

Maris shook her head. "Watch and learn." She turned toward the hallway and raised her voice. "I'm thirsty!"

As soon as they heard her declaration, two jocks rushed toward the vending machine — the winner of the race gave the machine a heavy whack on its side, and a soda fell out.

"Addie's thirsty, too," Maris added.

The second jock banged on the other side of the machine, and another soda popped out. He handed it to me with an adorable smile. It would have been rude not to accept it, right? So I just thanked him and smiled back. You know, just to be polite.

Suddenly, the bell rang, and I remembered I was supposed to be in math class — which happened to be all the way on the other side of the school. I took off toward the classroom, but Maris grabbed my arm and pulled me to a stop.

"Addie, Populars never run," she chided me.

Are you kidding me? Getting free sodas was one thing, but no way was I getting a detention just because Maris was afraid I'd wrinkle my skirt. "If Brandywine catches — uh-oh . . . incoming."

Principal Brandywine zoomed toward us on her scooter, her face twisted into an ugly scowl. Detention, here I come.

"Hello, Principal Brandywine," Maris greeted her, in the most sickeningly sweet voice I'd ever heard. "So sorry we're still in the hall."

And then, the strangest thing happened. I mean, stranger than the time Zach's new organic shampoo made all his hair fall out. Stranger than the green stuff growing under Ben's bed.

Principal Brandywine smiled.

I almost fell over, but Maris just smiled back, as if this kind of thing happened to her all the time. And I was beginning to think that maybe it did.

"Don't worry, child," Principal Brandywine said in a soft, kind voice. Had aliens invaded while I wasn't paying attention? Was Principal Brandywine a pod person, some kind of zombie with a human face and an alien brain? It was the only explanation I could come up with for her behavior. "You'll get there when you get there. And thank your mother for the lovely brooch." She straightened a giant gold-and-green turtle pin that was clipped to her lapel. "How did she know I collect turtles?"

Principal Brandywine took off down the hall in her scooter, giving us a cheery little wave. I gaped at Maris, who faced me head-on, totally unashamed.

"That is — so unfair," I sputtered. "Unless . . ." I stopped to think for a moment — if people want to do nice things for you, is that really so wrong? I mean, wouldn't it be even more wrong to turn them down, just because they don't treat everyone else the same way? Wouldn't that just hurt their feelings? Besides, what the rest of the kids didn't know wouldn't hurt them, right? "Unless . . . you're popular. And then —" I had to admit it. "It's pretty cool."

Maris just smiled, as if to say this was only the beginning.

And she was right.

My locker had never felt so small. But after seeing Maris's life of luxury, how could I go back to my sad little single-locker existence now that I knew how the other half lived?

As I was stuffing my books in, wondering how I'd never before noticed these inhuman conditions, some-one tapped me on the shoulder. *Who would dare sneak up on me? A Popular?* I thought. I whirled around — oh. It was Geena.

"I have *so* much to tell you about the AV Geeks," she gushed. "Did you know Harold can install a camera into a pen? Wild."

I gave her a weak smile. Did she seriously expect me to care what Harold the AV Geek could do? But then I reminded myself that not everyone was lucky enough to be a Popular. I smiled wider, resolving to be more under-standing.

"Ready to hit *Juice!?*" Geena asked, when I didn't say anything.

"Sorry, I can't," I told her. "I promised Maris I'd go to L.G.E. with her."

Geena's face fell. "You're going to Lip Gloss Emporium? With *Maris?* Today?"

It wasn't until I heard the shock in her voice that I remembered our plans. I'd promised to go to L.G.E. with Geena that weekend — we'd been planning it forever.

But it's not like I could turn down Maris, not after she'd gone out of her way to invite me along. I mean, that would just be rude, right? Geena would understand.

"Yeah, it's kind of a private pre-opening thing," I explained quickly. (I decided it would be best not to mention the celebrities that Maris promised would be there.) "Her dad knew someone." (Maris's dad knew *everyone*.) "So I thought I'd go and scout it out so when we go on Saturday we'll know where the good aisles are." There, that was a brilliant idea — but would she buy it?

"Uh, yeah," Geena said dubiously. I guess not. "Okay, I guess —"

"Well, call me tonight and I'll tell you all about it," I chirped, before she could say anything else. I was late to meet Maris for our pre-L.G.E. manicure. She'd convinced some seventh graders to give us the full beauty treatment. Amazing!

And I took off. But I didn't get away fast enough, because I could still hear her mumbling sarcastically to herself. "No, it's okay, Addie. I don't want to go with you guys, anyway. I'm too busy taking tiny pictures with my camera pen."

There was a bright flash, then a yelp, and I suspected Geena had just taken an accidental and very unwanted close-up of her own face. But I didn't turn around. I had places to go, people to snub. And I knew Geena would get over the L.G.E. thing. After all, she was my best friend, wasn't she? She should want the best for me — and life with Maris meant nothing but the best.

For Dad, it was a typical night at home — he was sitting at the kitchen table, paying some bills. When he was done, he'd go stretch out on the couch and fall asleep while reading the newspaper. Just a typical night. But for Mom, this was a special, once-in-a-lifetime kind of night. Well, not once in a lifetime, but once in a very long time — since Ben almost never got sick. And a sick Ben meant a happy Mom.

"It's hard to see him so sick," Mom said, struggling to frown as she carried Ben's empty dinner tray back down to the kitchen. She finally gave up the battle and grinned. "But this is the first time he's let me call him Benjie since he turned twelve! Go up there and bring him some tea," she urged Dad. "He'll let you ruffle his hair!"

As she set down the tray, she sneezed, and Dad looked up in alarm.

"You feeling okay?" he asked. "You might be start-ing to get this bug yourself."

Before she could answer, she sneezed again.

"No, I'm fine," she protested, sounding kind of stuffy. "It's a sympathy sneeze. I'm gonna go back up and see if he wants to watch *Muppets Take Manhattan*. It was his favorite film when he was little."

That's when I walked in the door, fresh from my fabulous trip to Lip Gloss Emporium. You could tell because I was wearing this awesome new L.G.E. T-shirt. And also because I'd brought along a delivery guy to carry all my stuff for me.

"Mom, do you have any cash?" I asked breezily. "I have to tip Darryl."

Mom gave Darryl a quizzical look, but took a dol-lar from her purse and gave it to me. I stuck it in Darryl's open hand. He didn't move.

"Uh, Mom?" I prodded, tipping my head slightly toward Darryl. He was obviously waiting for more.

Mom handed over a few more bills, and I stuck them in Darryl's hand, one by one. By one. By one. Finally Darryl decided he had enough, gave me a curt nod, and walked out the door. I'd miss him — after all, like Maris always says, good help is hard to come by.

"Hey, the lip gloss was free," I said defensively, noticing that Mom was glaring at me. "And they're prototypes, which means Mar-Mar and I will be the first kids to wear the colors to school!"

"Mar-Mar?" Dad asked. He's always been a little . . . slow.

"We get free product; they get free advertising," I explained, repeating what Maris had told me back in the store, when we were both stuffing our carts. "You know what they say: A day on the lips of a popular kid is worth its weight in Golden Sunset gloss."

"Who says that?" Dad asked, wrinkling his face in confusion.

See what I mean? He just didn't get it.

Mar-Mar warned me that now that I was popular, some people from my old life might not understand the new me. It turned out she was right — but then, wasn't she always?

That night, I wrote a new song. This wasn't one of those times when I was upset and needed to play my guitar to help me clear my head. No, my head was totally clear and I knew exactly what I was doing. And I was so excited about my new life that I couldn't help it, I just had to sing:

I never had a thing for the popular crowd.
They picked on me and laughed a little too loud.
But now I've found . . .
On the other side, life is sweet.
And the lip gloss is all free!

"Hey!" I greeted Geena at her locker the next morning. I was wearing one of my new shades of lip gloss, and couldn't wait for her to notice how great I looked.

"Hey," she replied coolly, without meeting my eyes.

"Geena, it's cool," I assured her, looking up and down the hallways. "Eli's not around. We can talk for a few minutes."

"I called you last night," Geena said, her voice still icy. "You never called me back."

Oops.

"Sorry. I was up late IM-ing Maris. We —" I stopped abruptly, because I'd just spotted Maris on her way down the hall and . . . well . . . you know Maris. She feels pretty strongly that you shouldn't be seen talking to the wrong people. Not that Geena was — well, it's just, better safe than sorry. "Actually, I gotta go," I said, backing away.

"Why?" Geena asked. "You said yourself, Eli's not here."

"But that Mr. Ward is a sneaky one," I babbled. "He could have camera pens trained on us."

"Text me later, okay?" Maris said in passing. She gave Geena a glare and glided on down the hallway.

"Oh, I get it," Geena sneered, watching Maris float away. "You're embarrassed to be talking to a geek!"

I didn't know what to say. I mean, "embarrassed"? That was a little harsh. I was just . . . Fortunately, I was rescued from having to explain exactly what I was, as Zach strolled up to join us. Or should I say, the Future CEO of America formerly known as Zach. He still had the same face and all — but he was wearing a bow tie!

"What's the haps, chicas?" he asked, showing off his tie, as if forgetting that a few days ago he wouldn't have been caught dead in one. He used to call ties "pathetic badges of corporate America." "Like it? All the FCEOs of A are wearing them."

But I wasn't saved for long, because Geena didn't have any time or energy to spare on Zach's transformation — she was too busy obsessing over mine.

"You're acting like this assignment is real, and it's not," she snapped. "You're not really popular and Maris isn't really your friend."

Uh, excuse me? Was Geena actually trying to pretend she knew something about how popular people worked? She didn't know anything.

"It's real llama hair from organically raised llamas," Zach pointed out, fondling his tie. This time I was the one who ignored him.

"How do you know?" I asked Geena, an angry fire building in the pit of my stomach. What kind of friend was she, trying to ruin my new life? "You don't even know her. She's actually pretty cool. . . ."

"Cool? Right." Geena snorted in disbelief. "I don't remember you calling her cool when she pushed you into the water fountain and told everyone you wet your pants!"

"You guys remember that push-me-pull-you from Doctor Doolittle?" Zach babbled. He's always trying to calm Geena and me down when we fight — but this time, it wasn't going to work. "I always thought that was a llama. Y'know, except for the part where it had two heads. Funny thing about llamas —"

"You know what I think?" I interrupted, the truth suddenly hitting me. "I think you're jealous that Maris and I are hanging out together!"

Geena slammed her locker door shut. "Please," she retorted, her voice coated with sarcasm. "Hang out with her forever for all I care. Have fun being boring together!"

Boring?! Right. Like going to a star-studded pre-opening of L.G.E. was boring? Like sitting in the VIP area at lunch was boring? Like doing whatever I wanted, like ruling Rocky Road Middle School was boring? I never knew Geena was so limited . . . but I guess she was. And I guess I'd outgrown her.

"Hardly!" I shouted. "I'll be sure to send you a postcard from Fabulous!"

And I would. But instead of "Wish you were here," it would say "Glad I'm *not* there." Let Geena live her boring, unpopular life, hanging out with the rest of the boring, unpopular people. Thanks to Maris, I had better things to do — and a better friend to do them with.

When I walked into social studies the next day, I tried my best not even to look at Geena as I walked past her. I wanted to pretend she didn't exist.

And it worked — I didn't even see her. Unfortunately, that meant I also didn't see the extension cord she'd unrolled across the room and pulled taut just as I walked by. So when my foot got caught in the cord and I went *splat* on my face, in front of everyone, I didn't know what had happened.

Until I saw Geena, holding the end of the cord. And smirking.

"Careful, Addie," she said sweetly. "It's hard to kiss Maris's butt and watch where you're going at the same time."

I glared at her and wished I had the power to

shoot deadly laser beams out of my eyes. Then I realized, I had something almost as good.

"Eli!" I called loudly. "An AV Geek is trying to speak to me."

Bingo. Eli Pataki zoomed up to Geena and whipped out his pink pad.

"Where's your root beer now, Fabiano?"

She rolled her eyes as Eli handed her the pink slip, but the damage was done.

Maris helped me up off the floor — what are friends for, right?

"Come on," she said soothingly. "I know just what you need."

Maris somehow convinced our teacher to let us out of class (and it seemed like all she had to do was smile), and then she led me through the hallways of the school to a door I'd never noticed before. She pulled out a small silver key and opened it, revealing a small, immaculate yoga studio, complete with padded floor and walls covered with yoga posters.

Maris, of course, had a special pink yoga outfit. I just wore my gym clothes.

And Maris, of course, knew all the poses, and could hold them all, even the Scorpion, where you have to balance on your forearms and kick your legs up over your head. I could barely stand on one foot without falling over. But maybe I would learn.

"I can't believe you guys get to take yoga for gym credit," I said for the third or fourth time as I struggled to stretch my leg up over my head.

"I know it seems like making geeks cry doesn't affect me," Maris said serenely, "but I carry it in my back." She gracefully leaned forward into another position.

"Oh." I didn't know what I was supposed to say. This whole yoga thing was new to me — almost as new as the idea that Maris was an okay person and a friend. But that one I was finally starting to get used to.

"Not oh," she corrected me. "*Ohmmmm.*"

"Right. *Ohmmmm.*" I tried to clear my head of all thoughts, like Maris had taught me. Tried to focus on my muscles and my breathing. In . . . out . . . in . . . out . . . in —

But my mind just isn't built that way. And I couldn't stop thinking about the million things that were bothering me. Thing number one? Geena.

"Can you believe Geena?" The question burst out of me before I could stop myself. "She totally doesn't get it."

"They never do," Maris replied. She lifted her leg

behind her until her heel was practically touching the back of her head and I did my best to imitate her. But I'm afraid that while Maris looked like an eagle (at least I think that's what she said the pose was called), I probably looked more like a pigeon. "Addie, hardly anyone is born popular. Most of us *become* popular and, in doing that, leave behind old friends to make room for the new. Have you ever heard of Mary Ferry?"

Of course I had. Mary and her boyfriend, Duane, were quirky but nice. However . . . I got the sense that it might be better to pretend I hadn't heard of her.

"No," I lied.

"And why would you have?" Maris asked, as if she'd expected just that answer. I sighed quietly — I'd made the right decision. Hanging out with Maris was fun, but kind of stressful — every time I opened my mouth, I was afraid that whatever popped out might convince her that I was a loser, too. "She's a loser. But when I was young and foolish, we were best friends. Once I saw I had an opportunity to become a Popular, I had to dump her."

"That's kinda harsh," I said, without thinking. I mean, it was. But maybe I wasn't supposed to point that out.

"Silly Addie," Maris responded as I tried to get my

arms and legs untwisted from their pretzel-like position. "It's not easy being popular. You can't climb to the top without stepping on a few losers."

Maris shifted seamlessly into a new position — but when I tried to follow her, my legs were a little slower than the rest of me. And I fell over with a loud thump.

"Hmm," she breathed, her eyes closed. "I always feel so peaceful at the end of a meditation."

I just felt sore. And bruised. And a little unsure of what was going to happen next.

How many "losers" would I need to step on to get to the top? And how much did I want to be there?

So is anyone surprised that after all that mother-son bonding, Mom eventually caught Ben's flu? No, I didn't think so. By the middle of the week, they were side by side on the couch, wearing matching robes and surrounded by matching piles of snot-filled tissues. Dad, who'd taken on Mom's Florence Nightingale role, brought them each a bowl of soup.

"All right, here we are," he said soothingly, setting down the steaming bowls of alphabet soup on a tray in front of each patient.

"Are all the letters there?" Mom asked weakly.

"Yes, and I saw at least three *Sue's* in there when I was pouring," Dad assured her.

Mom smiled and took a small sip of the soup. "I don't know what we would do without you," she told him. (Though with her stuffy nose, it sounded more like "I dote dow whad we would do widoud you.")

"Well, one of us has to hold this house together," he said confidently.

And then he sneezed.

"No. No. No!" Dad stammered, his eyes widening in panic. "No, no, no. I'm gonna go eat a handful of vitamin C and do a sinus cleanse."

I passed him on my way into the living room. Although after one sniff, I was ready to turn around and follow him out.

"*Ew*," I complained. "This room smells like sick."

"Really? I lost my sense of smell hours ago," Mom mused, her eyes all zoned out and glassy from too much cold medicine. "Right before my need for personal hygiene. I think my will to live is next."

Ben blew his nose and sighed pitifully.

"I've lost ten pounds in snot alone," he observed. "Maybe I can move down a weight class in wrestling."

Okay — too much information. Gross.

"Where are you going, Addie?" Mom asked. I was surprised she still remembered I was in the room.

"I'm meeting Maris at *Juice!*," I told her, shining with pride that Maris was hanging out with me in public.

"Oh, right," Mom said, sinking back against the couch. "Mar-Mar."

I guess you could say Mr. Ward's experiment was working better than even he had expected. The cafeteria looked totally different from the way it had just a few days before. On Monday, the tables had been almost completely silent, as everyone just stared across the table at the people in their new clique. Nobody had anything to say to one another. But toward the end of the week, everything loosened up, and people really got into their new groups. You know, like me and Maris. Or Zach and the FCEOs of A. After a couple of days with them, he realized that it was destiny he'd been placed with them — this was his chance to educate corporate America. Or, at least, corporate America-to-be.

"See, in Denmark all the workers get paid summer vacation," he explained as the table full of future business leaders stared at him, fascinated. "Yet, even with long vacations, they still produce more —"

"— because happy workers are productive workers!" one of the FCEOs finished for him, his face lighting up with the revelation.

"By George, I think you've got it!" Zach crowed triumphantly.

Even Geena had found something to share with her fellow AV Geeks. Not that I was paying any attention to what Geena and her new geek friends were doing. That was all beneath the new popular me.

"Believe me, there's nothing geeky about the right accessories," Geena was explaining, showing off her new homemade extension-cord accessories.

"I *love* it," Cranberry said. Yes, even *Cranberry* had made peace with her time in geekdom. "Next we can make purses out of duct tape!"

But I was willing to bet that no one, at any table, was having as much fun as I was. Mar-Mar had given me a present that morning: a hot-pink, off-the-shoulder T-shirt that read BLOND. Because that's what we were. Well, okay, so my hair was more sandy than true blond, but blond was such a good color for a popular girl. So I was going with it. She had one, too, so we totally matched. It was awesome. There were a group of kids at our table, the others that Mr. Ward had designated Populars. But we weren't talking to them — it was obvious that they were just "popular" for a school assignment. It wasn't real; it wasn't in their blood. When the week was over, they would all go back to their normal, ordinary lives. But for me, it was different. It was real.

I had been a little nervous to bring Maris home with me. Maris's house was more like a mansion, and it was the cleanest place I'd ever been. Everything was exactly where it belonged, and everything matched. The walls were white. The carpets were white. The furniture was white. It looked like a museum — it looked like no one lived there. Compared to that, my house looked like a barn. I mean, I've always loved my house, but that night, walking in with Maris by my side, all I could see was the mess and the clutter. Our house definitely looked like someone lived there. And it was the people who lived there I was most afraid of — I just knew my parents would do something to embarrass me in front of Mar-Mar.

Well, I shouldn't have been scared.

I should have been terrified.

As we walked into the living room, Maris stopped short at the sight of my entire family wallowing in their sickness. They'd turned the living room into a doctor's office — it was piled high with tissues (new and used), discarded books and magazines were strewn all over the floor, and a humidifier was puffing away in the corner. And there were my parents and Ben sniffling, coughing, and wheezing under a giant pile of sweaty blankets.

"Hold your breath and don't make eye contact," I whispered to Maris, trying to pull her toward the stairs as quickly as possible.

"Addie! Can you bring us some soup?" Mom gasped, catching sight of us.

"Addie, will you fetch me another blanket from the cedar closet?" my dad whimpered in this pathetic little voice. "I'm so cold."

They reached out to us, and we shrank away, as if we were in one of those old horror movies and my family were zombies, trying to pull us into their world.

"Come on, come on," I urged Maris, pushing past my parents' outstretched arms.

Safe at last.

As Maris stepped into my room, I shut the door behind us and sagged against it in relief. For about ten seconds. Then I realized that the biggest challenge was still to come. This was my room, after all. You could tell a lot about a person from their room — and what would

Maris be able to tell about me? I looked around, at my flowered curtains and lavender bedspread. Did these say "popular"? Or "big loser"?

"So, this is my room," I finally said, holding my breath.

Maris looked unimpressed.

"Well, at least it's not full of disease," she allowed.

My room was healthy! That was something.

"You play the guitar?" she suddenly asked, sounding less bored than she had all afternoon.

"Yeah, a little," I admitted fearfully. Did that make me cooler, or less cool? This popular thing was so confusing! "I write my own songs." Should I have said that?

"Play one!" Maris cried.

"No, it's okay. . . ." I was horrified. No way was I playing one of my songs for Maris. She'd think they were totally stupid. That was baby stuff. I hadn't had any time to write new songs. *Popular girl* songs.

"Oh, please?" Maris begged. She grabbed my arm and tugged on it like a little child. "Please, please, please, please, please, please, please —"

"Okay, okay." It was the only way to get her to stop. I picked up my guitar and took a deep breath. "This one's about my brother's goldfish." I started strumming and, just like always, as soon as I was actually playing the guitar, I forgot where I was and who I was with. I just lost myself in the music.

Goldy, don't know why you left us in such a rush.
But, Goldy, I'll think of you every time I flush.

I stopped playing when Maris burst into laughter.
"That's so lame, it's almost funny," she giggled.
It wasn't supposed to be funny. And it definitely wasn't supposed to be lame. But Maris knew best. . . .
"Yeah," I agreed halfheartedly. "It's about . . . death. It's . . . supposed to be funny."
I was about to say something else, but my dog, nancy, padded in and flopped herself on the bed.
"That's the ugliest dog I've ever seen," Maris marveled.
nancy whimpered, as if she'd understood, and I was about to say something in her defense — nancy isn't an ugly dog. She's beautiful. Okay, so she's kind of a shaggy mutt, but she's also the smartest dog I've ever met.
I could have told Maris all of that . . . but I didn't. I

just stood there, silent, and tried to pretend that Nancy wasn't giving me a dirty look.

"Oh, my gosh," Maris said, choking on her laughter. She was holding a framed picture that she'd found on my dresser. "Is this Geena Fabiano?"

I peeked over her shoulder — it was Geena all right. She was seven years old, and she looked like this total geek: greasy hair parted down the center, thick glasses with Coke-bottle lenses, and the goofiest smile you've ever seen. It didn't look anything like Geena these days — but it reminded me of the way she'd looked when we first became friends, and how much fun we'd had together in those days.

"Yeah, isn't it funny?" I agreed, laughing along with Maris. "Geena always begs me to throw it away, but I love it."

"Addie, that's brilliant!" Maris exclaimed. "You really do have what it takes to be popular."

"I do?" I asked, totally thrilled. And totally confused.

"This will be hilarious! We'll blow up the picture and we'll hang it in the hallway at school!" Maris exclaimed, her eyes lighting up as she imagined the looks on everyone's faces as they gaped at the photographic evidence of Geena's geek days.

"I dunno," I said hesitantly. I was imagining the look on *Geena's* face when she realized I betrayed her and made a fool of her in front of the whole school.

"Oh, come on, it'll be fun!" Maris wheedled.

For a second, I wished that Nancy would jump up and start barking at Maris. I wished that, out of loyalty to Geena, Nancy would fly through the air and start slobbering all over Maris's face, until she screamed and ran out of the room, and out of my life. At the very least, I wished that I had the nerve to take the picture out of Maris's hands, put it back on my dresser, and tell her that there was no way she was showing it to the whole school.

Maris stood there expectantly, waiting for my answer.

I didn't say yes. I couldn't do that to Geena, my best friend.

But I didn't say no, either.

And when she took the picture out of its frame and slipped it into her pocket, I didn't say anything at all.

I wrote a new song that night, but I'm not very proud of it. And I wish that I'd never had to write it at all:

Why didn't I just say no?
I stood there and watched her go.
The picture will hang for the whole world to see.
I'm a chicken,
'Cause I was afraid, if it wasn't Geena . . . it would
be me.

I got to school early the next morning and waited by Maris's locker. I knew Maris wouldn't get there until just after the bell rang — but I needed the extra time. I was pretty nervous about what I was about to do, and I needed some time to psych myself up. But maybe that was a mistake, because waiting around for Maris, I just got more and more nervous. By the time she finally showed up, I was almost ready to explode.

"Maris, I'm glad I caught you before class," I said quickly as she checked herself out in her locker mirror and smoothed down her long blond hair. "About the picture of Geena —"

"Don't worry." Maris smirked. "Julian from the art lab has it all taken care of. It will happen after lunch, when everybody's in the hallway."

"What?" How had she made her horrible plans so

quickly? And how was I going to stop them? "No, I shouldn't have given you that picture," I protested. I couldn't stop imagining the look on Geena's face when she saw that photo blown up for the whole school to mock. I'd never be able to face her again. Which would probably be okay, because I'm sure she'd never *want* me to face her again. "Geena doesn't deserve that. Even if we aren't friends anymore."

Maris was barely paying attention.

"Um, did you not hear me before when I said it will be *hilarious*?" she scoffed.

"I'm asking you *as a friend* to give the picture back," I replied, losing my patience. We were running out of time. I had to make her understand.

"*Pfft*. Please." Maris burst into giggles. "We're not friends. You were just someone to hang out with for a week so I wouldn't fail Mr. Ward's class."

I froze. Literally. It felt like I was turning into ice, from my head down to my toes. I couldn't say anything to her. I couldn't even *think* anything. So I just stared. I could barely breathe. I'd thrown away everything — I'd thrown away *Geena*. And for what? To be a Popular? *We're not friends,* Maris had said. Duh. It seemed so obvious now. When it was too late.

Maris closed her giant locker and walked away,

leaving me there standing in the hallway, staring at the empty spot she'd left behind.

"I can't wait to tell Cranberry that you actually thought we were friends," she sputtered as she turned her back on me. "She will *die!*"

I know, I know. I shouldn't have been so stunned. I mean, I've known Maris for years — I should have known exactly what kind of person I was dealing with. I should never have gotten carried away with the free sodas and special treatment. I should never have betrayed my *real* friends for a dumb school project.

I didn't know if Geena would forgive me for the way I had acted — but at the moment, I had bigger problems. Or at least, *Geena* was going to have bigger problems, if I didn't find some way to stop Maris's evil plan.

Fortunately, after I was finished getting surprised, I got upset. Then I got angry. Then I got an idea.

And *then*, I went to go find Mary Ferry — it was time to get even.

I couldn't track down Mary Ferry until lunchtime, but then I finally found her. She was sitting alone at a table on the edge of the cafeteria, her nose buried in a math book.

"Well, hello, Mary Ferry," I said triumphantly,

sitting down beside her. There was no sign of Duane, which was good, since I needed a quiet conversation with Mary.

She looked at me in confusion. I didn't like to interrupt her studying but I had to have her help.

"I need to talk to you about Maris Bingham," I continued, my eyes narrowing as I pictured my target. "You were best friends, weren't you?"

"Not just BF," Mary corrected. "BFF. Or at least that's what I thought. But it was more than that. We were synchronized swimming partners. . . ." Her voice drifted off, and she smiled.

"So, what happened?" I pressed her. I didn't really have time for a stroll down memory lane.

"Well, one day she didn't show up to practice and I was worried, so I rushed back to school. She told me —" Mary looked down, and I'm not sure, but I think I may have seen a tear dripping from the corner of her left eye. "She told me I swam like a whale."

Ouch.

What could I say to that?

So I didn't say anything. I just hoped Mary Ferry would pull herself together. And a little piece of me was dancing for joy — because suddenly, I was pretty sure that Mary would be ready and willing to go along with my plan.

"That is, if whales couldn't swim," Mary mused, still thinking about her synchronized swimming style. "Which they *can*. So it really made no sense at all. But it didn't matter, 'cause everyone laughed, anyway."

A familiar trill of laughter drifted across the cafeteria, and I looked up, distracted. There was Geena, chuckling at something one of the AV Geeks had said. She looked so happy. And it was up to me to make sure she stayed that way.

I looked back at Mary, who was waiting calmly for me to explain why I'd started this whole conversation in the first place. I hoped she wouldn't be disappointed.

"I think maybe you can help me," I began, and laid out my plan for her.

Not only did she love it, not only did she instantly agree to go along with it, but she had some ideas of her own. This was going to be even better than I'd expected. It looked like, once again, Maris had misjudged someone. Turns out that beneath Mary Ferry's kind face and pleasant smile lay something far more dangerous than a whale: a shark.

Even though Mr. Ward's project was finally over, Zach was still hanging out with some of the FCEOs of A. He'd introduced them to his friends from the basketball team — and now that the FCEOs had stopped wearing suits and started dressing like normal kids, they all seemed to fit together pretty well.

"Chip, you're a pretty cool guy, once you lighten up a little," Mario commented, slapping one of the FCEOs on the back.

"Thanks, homeslice," Chip responded eagerly — he sounded like he'd found the phrase in a book called *How to Talk Like a Hip Teenager*. It wasn't working.

"That's a little *too* light," Zach cautioned. Then they all laughed, Chip included. It was nice to see that at least some good had come of Mr. Ward's project. Though I wasn't sure how everyone else had figured out how to add friends to their life — when all I seemed able to do was subtract them.

"Excuse me, everyone!" Maris shouted. She had positioned herself in the middle of the staircase, so everyone in the hall would have to look up at her. And she would look down on them. It was her favorite position. "Excuse me!"

The noisy crowd rushing through the halls gradually quieted down and turned to face Maris. I was toward the front of the crowd, holding my breath, and hoping that everything went smoothly.

"I thought you could all use a little after-lunch laugh," Maris announced smugly, "courtesy of *Geena Fabiano!*"

I shot a quick look at Geena, who seemed totally confused. Maris yanked a cord that was hanging down from behind the GO, BULLFROGS! banner.

She grinned as a giant, poster-size photo unfurled from behind the banner. She soaked in the roaring laughter of the crowd. Until, suddenly, she realized that they were all laughing at her. Maris whirled around to look at the picture she'd unveiled. Geena's geek phase was nowhere to be seen. Instead, it was a bigger-than-lifesize shot of a younger Maris, wearing a bathing cap, nose plugs, floaty arm bands, and a swimming tutu. She looked ready to go for the gold in synchronized swimming . . . in the Geek Olympics. Maris tugged at the picture, beat her fists against it, but she couldn't get it down.

"Don't look!" she shrieked, throwing herself in front of the humiliating image. "Someone bring me some scissors! Don't look!"

Except that, in real life, when Maris tugged on the cord, nothing happened. Nothing popped out — no embarrassing photo of Geena, no embarrassing photo of Maris. Nothing.

See, Mary Ferry gave me exactly what I'd been looking for. A picture that would embarrass Maris in front of the whole world. She would never live it down. And I could have put it up there for everyone to see . . . but then I'd be as bad as she was. And nothing was worth that. Maris was wrong. You don't have to be a jerk to be popular.

"Um, that wasn't funny," a jock pointed out. He grabbed his friends and headed down the hallway. The rest of the crowd began to wander away, too, in search of something more entertaining. Personally, I was pretty entertained by the sight of Maris on the stairwell, tearing her hair out in confusion.

"Where's the picture?" she whined shrilly, her voice rising to a pitch that I was pretty sure only my dog could hear.

"Good joke, Maris! Subtle," one of her nerd groupies complimented her. She inched away. This obviously wasn't the kind of attention she'd been hoping for.

Then Maris caught sight of someone who *did* matter to her. And who was about to be in big trouble. "Julian, where's my picture? Julian? Julian!"

I would have liked to follow along behind them and hear whatever excuse Julian came up with. I was really enjoying watching Maris have a total meltdown. But that would have to wait — I still hadn't finished cleaning up the mess I'd made for myself. And the most important part of my fix-it plan was still to come.

Geena was one of the last kids to leave the area — maybe because she was trying to figure out exactly what Maris had been planning. Finally, she shrugged and walked down the hall toward her locker. She passed right by me — but didn't say a word. She totally froze me out.

I couldn't blame her. I just hoped it wasn't permanent.

I stayed a few feet away and watched as she opened her locker. There was a little bag inside, and she pulled it out, opening the note tied to the front. I didn't have to get close enough to read what it said, because I already knew — after all, I wrote it.

I'd struggled to come up with a way to say everything I felt, to tell her why I'd acted the way I had, to remind her of how much our friendship meant to me. But in the end, I couldn't figure out how to get it down on paper. So I had to settle for something short but true:

Sorry. Addie.

Then I stuffed the bag full of all my L.G.E. lip gloss samples.

And I crossed my fingers it would be enough.

It was only a matter of time.

My dad got sick. My mom got sick. Ben got sick. I guess I'd been foolish to think I could escape — just another mistake I made that week. But after breathing the germ-infested air in my house all week, my mistake caught up with me.

Big-time.

My nose is stuffy, I sang hoarsely. I was stretched out in bed, propped up on a pile of pillows. And I barely had enough strength to hold the guitar.

My eyes are puffy.
Snot is in my head.
Oh, how I wish that I was dead.
It's what I deserve for being a jerk.
Every painful sneeze,
and every gross dry heave. . . .

"Wow. Fun song."

I looked up at the sound of the familiar voice, afraid my fever was making me hallucinate.

But no, there she was — Geena. And I was pretty sure she was real. She came into my room holding a stack of magazines, and Zach appeared just behind her. He was carrying a tray of chicken soup.

"Geena! Zach!" I cried (or at least I would have cried, if my scratchy voice could get above a whisper). "What're you guys doing here?"

"We brought provisions," Geena explained, her voice light and friendly as if nothing had ever happened between us. I suddenly felt a million times better — which meant I still felt too sick to move. "Trashy magazines are, like, required reading for sickies."

"And chicken alphabet soup," Zach added. "With all the letters."

"Thanks, guys. Listen, Geena — I have to tell you something." If I didn't say anything about Maris's plan, Geena might never find out. But if we were going to be friends again, I knew I had to be honest. "I gave Maris —"

"I know," Geena cut me off. She *knew?* And she had still come to my house to cheer me up? "Julian told me all about it."

I grabbed the picture of Geena from my nightstand — I'd gotten it back from Julian the day before and brought it home for safekeeping.

"Here." I handed it to Geena, who took one look

and shuddered. "It's my only copy. Except for the billboard-size one that I paid Julian to shred."

I gave Geena a tentative smile, and she grinned back. Then she ripped up the picture into tiny, tiny pieces.

"It's okay," she assured me. "We all get a little crazy when free lip gloss is involved."

I leaned my head back against my pillows, all the stress of the last few days suddenly draining out of me.

"My mom says I'm too sick this weekend to do anything," I told her. "So if you want to go to Lip Gloss Emporium without me —"

Geena just shrugged. "Hey, it'll still be there when you get better," she pointed out. "Unless Zach wants to scout it out with me beforehand?"

"Oh, yeah, okay," he said sarcastically. "Just as soon as you come with me to the moth sanctuary."

"As long as she can bring a can of Bug Kill," I teased.

Zach looked alarmed, until Geena elbowed him gently so he knew we were joking.

"I'm just kidding," I swore.

"Don't play with my emotions like that," Zach complained.

But I wasn't really listening — all this excitement had worn me out, and I was starting to feel a little woozy. It was too hard to focus on Zach and Geena's chatter, so instead I just concentrated on picking out letters in my alphabet soup.

"I think I see my name," I murmured to myself. Then I leaned back against my pillows and shut my eyes, just for a minute. I barely noticed when Geena and Zach slipped out, promising they'd be back again to visit the next day.

I smiled and knew that tonight, for the first time in days, I wouldn't have any trouble drifting off to sleep. Now that I was done being a Popular, and Zach and Geena were back in my life, I didn't have a worry in the world.

Well, except for the worry that on Monday, there would be a new school project to deal with. It's just a little too easy for me to get carried away — and you see what happens next! I mean, not that I believe in bad luck or anything — but after the science fair disaster, and Mr. Ward's fiasco — I had to wonder. Maybe when it came to school projects, I really was jinxed.

But you know what? I decided I wasn't too worried about that, either. And I'm still not. Because if I learned anything from both of these projects, it's that I can make it through anything, as long as I have Geena and Zach by my side.

And they stay by my side, no matter what. Which means that, jinx or no jinx, I'm pretty much the luckiest kid in the world.